FOCUS ON THE FAMILY®

Christian Heritage Series

THE CHICAGO YEARS

The Trick

Nancy Rue

BETHANY HOUSE PUBLISHERS
MINNEAPOLIS, MINNESOTA 55438

A Focus on the Family book
Published by Bethany House Publishers
A Ministry of Bethany Fellowship International
11400 Hampshire Avenue South
Minneapolis, Minnesota 55438
www.bethanyhouse.com

Printed in the United States of America by
Bethany Press International, Minneapolis, Minnesota 55438

Library of Congress Cataloging-in-Publication Data

Rue, Nancy N.
    The trick / Nancy Rue.
        p.   cm. — (The Christian heritage series. The Chicago years ; 1)
    Summary: In the 1920s, ten-year-old Rudy goes to Chicago to live with his rich Great-aunt Gussie, an imperious and outspoken woman dedicated to doing good works, and falls in with boy aspiring to become a mobster.
    ISBN 1–56179–734–0
    [1. Chicago (Ill.) Fiction. 2. Great-aunts Fiction. 3. Gangsters Fiction. 4. Christian life Fiction.] I. Title. II. Series: Rue, Nancy N. Christian heritage series. Chicago years ; 1.
PZ7.R88515Tt   1999
[Fic]—dc21
                                            99–19627
                                                CIP

00 01 02 03 04 05 /15 14 13 12 11 10 9 8 7 6 5 4 3 2

For Keith Wall—

*thanks for skipping
with me through the
Christian Heritage years.*

Chapter One

S o where *is* the old lady?" Rudy Hutchinson said.

His father sighed one of his Rudy-what-am-I-going-to-do-with-you sighs that came all the way from his knees. Rudy's twin sister, Hildy Helen, poked Rudy between his first and second ribs—her favorite spot for poking.

"What?" Rudy said innocently. "What did I say?"

Their father, Jim Hutchinson, was already back to his own thoughts as he gazed vaguely around bustling Union Station. Hildy Helen shook her head at Rudy.

"As if you didn't know what," she said. "You know he doesn't want us calling Aunt Gussie 'the old lady.' "

"Well, isn't she?" Rudy said. He gave the glob of dark brown curls that always dangled in the center of his forehead a toss, and, shoving it back, returned his tweed cap to its place. His head was sweaty in the Chicago heat, but Rudy *always* wore a cap. The bill was good for hiding the mischief in his close-set brown eyes.

"Sure she's old," Hildy Helen said. "Dad says she must be in her sixties by now."

"And she's a lady, right?"

"With all her money, I guess she *is!*" Hildy Helen flipped back her braid of chocolate-brown hair, as straight as Rudy's was curly,

1

and watched a young woman of about 20 hurry by with her skirt teasing around her knees. Hildy's almost-as-brown-as-Rudy's eyes followed her wistfully. "I sure hope Aunt Gussie's modern," she said. "You would think she would be. I mean, Dad says she's on every committee. Did you know she was very important in getting women the right to vote?"

"Swell," Rudy said.

"Anyway, even if she *is* practically ancient, I'm sure she's very progressive." Hildy glanced at her father out of the corner of her eye. "I bet she even has her hair bobbed."

"Here we go again," Rudy said.

He watched his father return Hildy's glance from round, rimless glasses. Dad had small, dark eyes, like Rudy's, and when he was really paying attention, they snapped like tiny firecrackers. "No hair-bobbing," Dad said, then went back to squinting across the terminal for some sight of his Aunt Gussie.

"Then what was the point of moving here anyway?" Hildy Helen said to Rudy, her lip sticking out in a pout.

"I don't know," Rudy said. "I never wanted to come in the first place."

Hildy Helen moved her big eyes to her brother. They were spaced farther apart than his, which gave her a softer look. But Rudy had never thought of his sister as being anything *close* to "soft." She could out-talk him, out-run him, and sometimes out-wrestle him. Right now, he knew she was about to out-think him. She loved to "discuss."

"You really would rather have stayed in Shelbyville?" she said. "Dumb old Indiana?"

"Yeah. It was boring, but at least I knew everybody."

"You knew who you could give the business to, is what you mean," Hildy Helen said.

Rudy shrugged, but he knew Hildy didn't miss the smirk that was twitching at the corners of his big-grin mouth. "You remember how I could steal a pickle right out of the jar on Old Man Young's counter *every day*, and he never caught me?" he said.

"Uh-huh."

"And the way Miss Cross-Eyes thought I was so sweet to bring her an apple on Mondays—when every one of them had a worm in it? And she never said a word?"

"Don't let Dad hear you call her 'Miss Cross-Eyes,' " Hildy Helen said.

"You laughed every time I called her that."

Hildy Helen laughed now, a husky giggle that always sounded like she was about to cough. "I know. You always make me laugh."

Rudy nodded at her, as if he'd just made some important point.

"What?" Hildy Helen said.

"Look around you. Do you see anything here that's going to make you laugh?"

His eyes followed hers, both of them taking in the high-ceilinged train station. The walls were made of Indiana limestone—he had recognized that right away. But besides that, there was nothing at all here that even resembled their life in the country with their small-town lawyer father and their procession of various nannies and housekeepers, who always quit before the twins could drive them completely crazy.

No, this building was immense and boasted a grand staircase and tall, thick columns with fancy plasterwork at their tops and a marble floor that echoed the steady clatter of rushing feet.

Rudy had never seen so many folks in one place, and every one of them were sober-faced and seeming to have somewhere important to be and almost certainly something equally important to do. Rudy had neither of those—because except for the fact that he was in Chicago, he didn't know exactly where he was going or what he was going to do when he got there. That gave him a churning, uneasy feeling inside, and there was only one thing to do when he felt that way.

"This place is only three years old," Hildy Helen was saying. "Did you know it took them 10 years to build it?" She brought her eyes down from the glass ceiling that curved above them for what seemed like miles. "They started it in 1915, and—"

She stopped, and her eyes narrowed. "What are you thinking, Rudy?" she said.

"Oh, nothing."

"Liar."

"Am not."

She folded her hands across the front of the shapeless, mid-calf, brown dress she was wearing—the one she'd told Dad was too old-fashioned for words and that she was going to be mortified to be seen in on the streets of Chicago—and surveyed Rudy closely.

"Yes, you are," she said. "You're up to something. What is it?"

"Nothing," Rudy said again. He picked up his drawing pad, which he'd laid on the bench next to him, and took his pencil to it. Hildy glanced at it and shook her braid with a vengeance.

"That isn't what you're up to," she said. She gave a soft snort. "You could do cartoons of Mickey Mouse with your eyes closed. Come on—what?"

She was right, of course. He'd gazed at the poster for *Plane Crazy* a thousand times when the movie came to Shelbyville. But he took his time finishing one of Mickey's ears while Hildy Helen huffed and puffed. When he knew she was just about to give up and walk away, he stuck his pencil inside the pad, looked up at her with a grin, and said, "Meet me outside the men's washroom in five minutes."

Her eyes sparkled to life. "Why?" she asked.

"You'll see."

"I'm not coming unless you tell me why," she said.

But Rudy took off across the terminal, still grinning. He knew she'd come anyway. Of course, she'd tell herself she wasn't going to, that this was just another one of Rudy's pranks. But then, he knew, she'd give in and she'd be there because she couldn't stand to miss out on anything—even if the joke turned out to be on her.

The trick itself was still taking shape in his mind as his engineer-style boots clunked clumsily across the shiny floor. He'd already played every prank in the book on his sister in their 10-year lifetime—the best being the time he rolled her down a hill in an old tire, the most recent being the carefully placed itching powder in her underwear drawer. Unfortunately, his itching powder was packed in his trunk at the moment. But Rudy could always think of something, and he was thinking of it now.

Here's the plan, he told himself. *Find a good place to hide. When she gets to the door of the men's washroom, jump out and shove her inside!*

It wasn't the best prank he'd ever come up with, but it was all he could think of in unfamiliar surroundings. And the good hoot he was going to get out of it was bound to help him get rid of the uneasiness that was churning in him like a tidal wave.

The challenge was to find a place to hide. Rudy gave the terminal a quick once-over from under the brim of his cap. He located the washroom easily. There was a balcony above the front door, but that was too far from the washroom. There were also some fancy light poles placed about, but they were too skinny to conceal even his average 10-year-old form. Hildy would have said she could *never* hide behind one of those, not with her "thick body." Rudy didn't see a thing wrong with her body, but she was always raving on about how all the flappers were so slender and—

He shook his head. The only trouble with Hildy Helen was that she talked too much and crowded his thinking. He glanced up at the clock and scanned the station once more.

And there it was, the perfect hiding place. A long wooden bench just about six feet from the washroom. There was a man sitting on it, but he was sleeping under his straw bowler, so hard, in fact, that his snoring was stirring the neatly folded points of the handkerchief that stuck up out of his suit pocket. If Rudy hadn't been in such a hurry, he might have found some pepper to sprinkle on that hanky.

But there wasn't much time. Hildy Helen would be deciding to head for the washroom right about now, and he needed to be well out of sight.

With a quick look over his shoulder to be sure she hadn't spotted him, Rudy dropped to his knees and then to his stomach. With a wriggle that pulled one of his suspenders off his shoulder, he slid under the bench like a lizard and turned himself around so he could watch.

There wasn't much to see but feet, but that was enough. Amid the men's white spats and the women's shiny patent leather pumps, it would be easy to spot Hildy Helen's laced-up high-tops, the ones she'd wailed to Dad needed to be replaced by a shiny pair of Mary Janes with a strap.

And there they were, making their way deftly through the crowd, straight for the men's room. It was so delicious, Rudy could hardly contain himself.

The only thing that would make this better would be if the washroom was just full *of men,* he thought. It was worth a look-see.

He stretched his neck some, remembering to snatch off his cap, and got his head partway out from under the bench. He was almost trod on by a pair of calf oxfords, but to his delight they, too, pointed in the direction of the washroom. Rudy looked up at the man's gray flannel trousers and grinned. This was surely a no-nonsense city man who wasn't going to take kindly to finding a squealing girl next to the toilet.

He pulled his head back under the bench and gave the man time to reach his destination.

Get ready, Hildy Helen! Rudy thought. The thrill of evil tingled up his backbone, replacing the ripple of uneasiness in his stomach. *One, two, three—go!*

He thrust his head from under the bench, grinning for all he was worth. But he felt the smile freeze as if he'd just stuck his lips to a block of ice. Right there, just a quarter of an inch from the tip of his nose, was the blue-steel barrel of a pistol.

✝ ✝ ✝

Chapter Two

I t was a real gun all right. Rudy had never seen one in real life, but he'd looked at enough posters for Tom Mix movies to know he could be knocked right off a horse—or out from under this bench—if the person holding it pulled the trigger. It was time for an emergency prayer.

God, help, please! he prayed. *I'm in trouble again. I'm sorry. I'll never play another joke as long as I live. Just, please, help!*

Then he squeezed his eyes shut and waited, his heart slamming inside his chest like a sledgehammer.

"Nice and quiet, and nobody gets hurt," he heard a man say. Whoever he was, the man talked as if he had a mouth full of marbles.

Rudy answered in an obedient whimper, "Yes, sir."

"Let's go."

Rudy opened his eyes and started to wriggle out from under the bench. But the feet in front of him, clad in mirror-bright, black patent leather shoes, were pointed sideways from him, right behind two more feet that peeked their brown leather noses out from under a pair of baggy trousers. Both sets of shoes began to shuffle forward. The gun barrel was still there, but as the two men moved, the pistol disappeared—and so did the feet.

It took a full 30 seconds for Rudy's mind to start working again. *He wasn't pointing it at me!* Rudy realized. *He didn't even know I was here. I'm alive! I'm alive!*

He was close to springing out from under the bench and announcing that fact to the entire station when he heard a sharp sound, and then another, and still another. The only things he'd ever heard like it were firecrackers—the ones he and Hildy Helen had set off outside Farmer Cole's chicken house last year.

But Farmer Cole's chickens had never squawked like the women in Union Station did just then. The terminal's rock walls rang with terrified screaming, and all Rudy could see from under the bench were mobs of feet, tearing by in confused pairs. One set of high-tops skidded under the bench beside him, and Hildy Helen was suddenly tugging at his arm.

"What happened?" Rudy said.

"A man just got shot!" she said. "Right outside the door—right out on the sidewalk!"

"Liar!" Rudy said.

"Am not! Everybody started screaming and running and hiding, so I thought I ought to, too."

Rudy grinned. "Did you scream?"

"No, I did not." She squirmed into a more comfortable position. "It didn't even seem real. At first I thought somebody was playing a joke."

"It was real all right," Rudy said. His heart had slowed down, and he was starting to enjoy himself. "I saw the gun. They were right here—right by this bench!"

"Lucky!" Hildy Helen said. "You always have all the fun."

"You gotta stick with me, kid."

"You're the one who told me to go away and meet you in five minutes. I'm not falling for any more of your tricks, Rudy Hutchinson."

Her voice choked off into a squeak, and Rudy himself let out a squeal. Two large, thick hands were suddenly fumbling under the bench, and before Rudy could scramble backward out of their grasp, one of them had latched on to his suspender and was pulling him forward. From the sound of Hildy's shrieks, she was getting the same treatment.

"Don't hurt me!" Rudy cried. "I didn't see a thing! I swear!"

The man with the thick hands obviously didn't believe him, because he kept pulling until the twins were on their feet, more or less. Then his hands went to their backs, and he thrust the two of them forward.

Rudy's heart picked up its sledgehammer beat again, and he could barely think to get out an emergency prayer. Beside him, Hildy Helen was squalling like a starving calf.

"D-ad! Help! We're being kidnapped!"

People passing barely glanced at them from under their cloche and fedora hats and kept going, still shaken from the sound of gunshots. Mr. Thick Hands kept walking, too. While Hildy Helen kept screaming, Rudy froze.

It's all over, he thought, terrified. *God knows that I'll never give up playing tricks on people, and He's just going to let me die. This is the guy with the gun, and he thinks I saw the whole thing, and he's going to take us both out and kill us!*

All Rudy could do was hang his head and let the man drag him across the terminal to his death. He opened his eyes for one last look at the world, but with Mr. Thick Hands holding him by the scruff of the neck like a puppy, all he could see were the marble floor and the man's brown high-topped shoes.

Brown high-topped shoes.

Not black patent leathers with pointed toes.

Rudy came to life in a rally of wiggles. "He's not the guy!" he shouted to Hildy Helen. "He's not the one!"

"Well, he most certainly is," said a voice as crisp as a starched shirt. "Put them down, Sol. If it's safe out there now, you can take the bags out to the car."

Hildy Helen stopped screeching and stared at a tall, lean woman who was staring back at her out of round, wire-rimmed spectacles. Rudy joined in the staring as the woman put out her hand to Hildy Helen and said, "Hello, Hildegarde. I am your Aunt Gustavia. Hildegarde Gustavia, to be precise. You may call me Aunt Gussie."

Rudy wanted to call her *Sergeant* Gussie. She stood straighter than a wooden toy soldier, and her gray hair was pulled back so tightly into a bun at the nape of her neck, Rudy was sure she couldn't move her head even if she tried.

She seemed to be doing a full inspection of Hildy Helen as Hildy shook her hand. Their aunt's small dark eyes moved up and down shrewdly, as if she were checking things off on a list. And Hildy, Rudy knew, was inspecting her right back and probably not liking what she was seeing.

Aunt Gussie was dressed all in gray, except for the black-strapped pumps and the white collar and gloves. Even her black-banded, wide-brimmed hat was an exact match for her gray hair, which was very definitely not in a bob. Her skirts hung stiffly about her ankles. She couldn't have been less modern if she'd been Cleopatra. It brought a smirk to Rudy's face.

Aunt Gussie wiped it off with a glance. "And you are Rudolph," she said in her crackling-with-starch voice.

"Rudy," he said.

All right, he thought quickly as he returned her handshake. *This one's going to take some work, but I can do it. I can always do it.*

Rudy turned to his father with a grin. "Jeepers, Dad," he said. "She's a lot prettier than you said she was!"

"James Hutchinson," Aunt Gussie said without taking her eyes from Rudy, "you have either taken to lying your fool head off, or I must get you to an eye doctor immediately."

Dad ran a weary hand through his graying reddish-brown hair. "My eyes are fine," he said. "It's Rudy's that needs some attention."

Rudy gave Aunt Gussie his best smile, the one that always nudged fat Mrs. Drexel at the candy store in Shelbyville to slip an extra licorice into his bag. It had no effect on Aunt Gussie. She turned briskly away from him and toward Mr. Thick Hands, who had a thick face, too, under his shock of white hair. He was wearing a dark green uniform, even in the muggy summer heat, but he stood, his cap in his hands, without dropping an ounce of sweat.

"Have you loaded the bags, Sol?" Aunt Gussie said in a loud voice.

"Yep," Sol said.

"Then what are we standing around for?"

"Don't know," Sol said. He turned on his heel and marched toward the door. His back was as straight as Aunt Gussie's, in spite of the fact that he must have been 75 years old if he was a day.

"I didn't know old Sol was still around," Dad said as he offered Aunt Gussie his arm.

She curled a white-gloved hand around his elbow and gave a curt nod. "He'll never die," she said. "He's too ornery. Come along, children."

With that, she steered Dad to the door. Rudy looked at Hildy Helen, and he was sure he had never seen her more disappointed. Her mouth was in a wiggly line all the way across her face.

"I don't think she's very modern," she said.

"Modern?" Rudy said. "I'd settle for 'nice.' We've had schoolteachers who looked friendlier than she does."

"Schoolteachers?" Hildy Helen said with a snort. "Farmer Cole has *bulls* that are friendlier!"

"How 'bout mother sows?"

"No, geese—those ones with the big bumps on their bills!"

That discussion carried them out into the glaring afternoon light, where the sight of Aunt Gussie's car grabbed Rudy's attention. Ah, now here was an opportunity.

"Is this a Pierce Arrow, Aunt Gussie?" he said, though he knew it was. He loved to look at pictures of cars in magazines and then draw them.

"That it is," Aunt Gussie said.

"That's a fine automobile, ma'am."

"I know it, or I wouldn't have wasted my money. As it was, I just gave up my horse and buggy five years ago. I wouldn't have been caught dead in one of those ridiculous Model T's."

Rudy grinned at her. "Why is a Model T Ford like a bathtub, Aunt Gussie?" he said.

She twitched an eyebrow.

"Because nobody wants to be seen in one!" he said.

Aunt Gussie rewarded him with a sniff and disappeared into the backseat of the long, sleek black Pierce Arrow. Hildy Helen poked him in the rib. "I don't think she thought that was funny," she said.

"Huh," Rudy said. "I could have gotten a *prune* to laugh at that."

"Get in," Dad said. "I'll ride up front with Sol."

At least Dad hadn't suggested that Rudy sit up there. It would be pretty hard to carry on a conversation with old, hard-of-hearing Pudding Face—although Rudy wasn't all that excited about talking with Aunt Gussie, either. So far, none of his most charming tricks were working on her.

Hildy Helen seemed reassured by the handsome car and by the busy, modern city they wove their way through on the way to Aunt Gussie's. But it made Rudy's stomach churn.

It was so crowded, for one thing, and not just with people,

although human beings did clog the sidewalks and the intersections in a hurried mass. It was the buildings that made Rudy feel as if there weren't room to breathe—all of them hulking over the streets like green and gray and blue giants of granite and iron and steel. He could see why they called them "skyscrapers."

"What's that river?" Hildy Helen said as they cruised across a bridge.

"The Chicago, of course," Aunt Gussie said. "Hasn't your father told you about the city?"

"Just that he grew up here with you," Hildy Helen said.

"Well, pay attention then," Aunt Gussie said. "There is likely to be an examination later on."

"You mean, a test?" Rudy said.

Aunt Gussie didn't answer but pointed a long finger out the side window. "In that direction is what we call the North Side," she said. "That's where the wealthy live, in their brownstones and high rise apartment buildings."

"So that's where *you* live," Hildy Helen said. "Dad did tell us you were filthy rich."

"I never used the word *filthy*!" Dad said from the front seat.

"Yes, Hildegarde, I am somewhat wealthy—but I refuse to live among those North Side Gold Coast snobs."

"Oh," Hildy Helen said. Her face was falling again.

"Behind us is the West Side," Aunt Gussie continued. "Most of the ethnic neighborhoods are there. It's largely industrial."

Rudy had no idea what 'ethnic' or 'industrial' meant, and he didn't feel like asking. There seemed to be cars coming at them from all sides, and they were making his stomach churn even harder.

"I, and now you, live on the South Side," Aunt Gussie went on, tapping her glove against the window on her right. "The place where all three areas come together is called the Loop—which we're about to enter."

Rudy hadn't thought it was possible for the city to get louder, but as they drove into "the Loop"—a mass of traffic and more giant buildings—the sounds of horns and trains and voices rose to a deafening din that made Rudy put his hands over his ears.

"There's a train up above us!" Hildy Helen cried out over the noise.

"It's called the 'El,'" Aunt Gussie said matter-of-factly, as if she didn't notice the string of railroad cars that was sailing over their heads. Rudy ducked.

"Those tracks are what makes it a loop," Hildy Helen said.

"Very observant," Aunt Gussie said, clicking her tongue. "James, I was beginning to think you'd raised a pair of country bumpkins."

Rudy tried the charming grin again. "I ain't no country bumpkin, ma'am," he said. "Whatever give ya that idea?"

Aunt Gussie shuddered and went back to the tour. Rudy shrugged and looked out the window.

It felt as if they were driving straight into a machine with everything crisscrossing—the cars, the people on foot, and the trains rattling both above and beneath them. And it was all so sharp—the corners of the buildings and even the way the sun cut in where it could in long, hard shafts.

"Well, I'm sure it's modern," Hildy Helen said. "But it isn't a very *pretty* place."

"It's pretty enough when you get down to the lake," Aunt Gussie said, pointing straight ahead.

"What lake?" Rudy said.

Aunt Gussie erupted like a teakettle with a head of steam. "James Hutchinson, for heaven's sake!" she said. "What have you been doing with these children?"

"Trying to keep them from killing their nannies," Dad said dryly. "There hasn't been much time for geography."

"I'll have to see to it," Aunt Gussie said. "But not today. You must get settled in first."

Hildy Helen wrinkled her nose, and Rudy took in a sniff, which nearly left him gagging.

"What is that smell?" Hildy said.

"You didn't wash your teeth this morning, Hildy?" Rudy said.

"That would be the Union Stockyard," Aunt Gussie said as Sol turned the car and headed right into the strong animal odor. "They cover 500 acres of South Side real estate."

"The smell hasn't changed a bit," Dad said, giving his first chuckle of the afternoon. "It makes you feel alive, doesn't it?"

"It makes me feel dirty!" Hildy Helen said.

"It makes me feel like I'm going to throw up," Rudy said. "Quick, somebody open a window!"

"There will be no regurgitation in my automobile, Rudolph," Aunt Gussie said. "Kindly restrain yourself."

"It was just a joke," Rudy muttered. But he guessed there would be no *joking* in Aunt Gussie's automobile, either.

✝ ✝ ✝

unt Gussie kept droning on, as if everyone in the car were completely absorbed in her every word. Hildy Helen was making more of an effort than Rudy to pay attention.

"I don't suppose your father has told you about the railroads, the lumberyards, and the mail-order houses, either," Aunt Gussie said. "Those are the things that make Chicago prosper."

"Aunt Gussie's husband, Karl Nitz, made his fortune in lumber," Dad said, as if he were trying to make up for his failure to educate them.

"And surely your father has neglected to tell you about the new opera house," Aunt Gussie went on. "It's bigger than the Metropolitan Opera in New York."

Rudy lost the rest of the conversation in the smoke and the steam that hung over them as they drove toward the South Side, closer to the smell of burning coal and the stink of the stockyard. If he hadn't been crazy about the idea of coming here before, he absolutely hated it now.

I wish I had put up a bigger fight, he thought.

But at the time their dad had sat the twins down a few months ago and told them that Aunt Gussie, the aunt he'd grown up with in Chicago, wanted them all to move in with her in her mansion on Prairie Avenue, Rudy had just said he didn't see what was the matter with the life they had now.

Their mother had died in the influenza epidemic of 1918, when he and Hildy Helen were just babies, but they got along all right. There was usually a nanny or a housekeeper until the twins got out of hand. And when there wasn't one, he and Hildy Helen looked after themselves.

But Dad had pointed out that he was restless with his small-town law practice and he wanted to make a difference in someone's life—not just handle cases like Farmer Cole accusing Farmer Jenson of stealing one of his turkeys.

"The times are changing, and not entirely for the better," Dad had said. "I want to be able to help people when change affects them."

"Why can't you do that here?" Rudy had said.

Because, Dad told them, Aunt Gussie had offered to set him up in a practice where he could do what was called *pro bono* work, which meant taking the cases of people who couldn't afford to pay him. And Aunt Gussie was certain the children could benefit from living in her house, getting a city education, and having social opportunities, just the way their father had.

Rudy would have kept on arguing, if it hadn't been for Hildy Helen. Those "social opportunities" had pricked up her ears like she was a bird dog on a trail.

"Aunt Gussie is modern. I know she is!" Hildy Helen had told him. "Let's go, Rudy! We'll have such fun!"

But so far, this wasn't Rudy's idea of a good time. And things didn't look up when Sol turned the Pierce Arrow into a neighborhood that was as silent and empty as the city was noisy and hustling.

"My stars," Dad said.

"I told you the place was different," Aunt Gussie said.

Their father looked stunned. "You didn't tell me just *how* different," he said.

"I'm glad to know it didn't always look like this," Hildy Helen whispered to Rudy as they climbed out of the car in front of a large brick house with an imposing front door that at once made Rudy think of some kind of fortress. Rudy nodded.

"No kidding," he said. "I mean, that's a mansion, all right—"

"But the neighborhood is a dump!"

She was right. Although the street was wide and lined with thick-trunked trees, there was none of the "gracious living" Dad had always spoken of when he'd talked about his days here on Prairie Avenue. There were some other big, old houses up and down the street, but most were boarded up, and the rest looked as if they ought to be. Between them were gaping vacant lots with only the decaying remains of the homes that once stood there. The whole place had a left-behind feeling that made Rudy feel empty inside. He immediately threw back his head and laughed.

"What?" Hildy Helen said.

"We're going to have some kind of opportunities here," he said, "living in the slums."

"Come along—don't stand out here gawking," Aunt Gussie called to them.

"That's right!" said another voice. "Dinner's ready! It's *been* ready. And it's gonna be one dried-up mess if somebody don't eat it!"

Rudy and Hildy Helen gaped at a very tall black woman who stood towering in the doorway, yelling out at them with a voice that could have belonged to a man. It was enough to get Rudy hustling toward the front door.

When he got there, Aunt Gussie shooed him inside with Hildy Helen on his heels and said, "Quintonia, this is Hildegarde, my namesake, and Rudolph. Children, this is Quintonia. She runs the house, and don't you forget it."

"Quintonia?" Dad said. "Quintonia Hutchinson?"

The woman nodded and broke into a big grin, showing over-sized, white teeth with a wide space between the two middle ones.

"You're Reverend Henry James's youngest!" Dad said. "I remember you!"

"As well you should," said Aunt Gussie. "You two got into enough trouble together as children."

Rudy felt himself brighten. "You did? What kind of trouble?"

Quintonia's smile twisted into a scowl. "You ain't never gonna hear about none of it from me," she said. "Now, is this dinner gonna get eaten, or am I gonna have to feed it to Picasso?"

"We're coming along right now," Aunt Gussie said. She led the way up a short flight of wide stairs into a large, paneled entrance hall. Before he could even ask who Picasso was, Rudy stopped so short that Hildy Helen walked up the back of his leg.

"Would you look at this?" he whispered to her as Aunt Gussie stalked off into another room with Dad after her.

"Oh, my," was all Hildy Helen could say.

The hallway was immense, and it led to an impressive staircase carpeted with a brightly colored rug that was surely from the Orient, but that wasn't what had them standing there with their mouths hanging open. It was just that there wasn't a single space anywhere in the great hall—not an inch of the shelving that ran all the way around close to the ceiling or a top of a polished table or a square foot of a shiny wood wall—that wasn't covered in something. And everything was so exotic and foreign-looking and strange.

"What *is* all this stuff?" Hildy Helen whispered.

Rudy picked up what appeared to be a drum. The wooden, carved figure that had been holding it toppled over onto the table. Rudy gave the drum a thump.

"This is pretty swell," he said.

"Look at this." Hildy Helen was holding a mask in front of her face, a frightening looking thing made of shells.

"That's nothin'." Rudy made a dive for a brass stool shaped like a crocodile. He sat down in a nearby chair, put his foot on the stool, and immediately began to slide down the chair yelling, "Help, Hildy! It's getting me! It's eating me!"

"What on earth is going on out here?"

Aunt Gussie's crackling voice brought both of them to a giggling halt. Hildy Helen plastered her hands over her mouth, and Rudy felt himself turning purple from holding his breath. Behind Aunt Gussie, Dad was turning a shade of purple himself.

"James," Aunt Gussie said, "do your children always behave this way in someone's home?"

Dad coughed. "They've just never been in a home quite like this one, Auntie," he said.

Rudy gave charm one more stab. "You have such interesting *things*, Auntie!" he said. "Was this once a real alligator?"

"Yes, and she had it brassed, which is the same thing she's going to do to you if you don't keep your hands off her artifacts," Dad said. His eyes were twinkling behind his glasses. Aunt Gussie's, however, did not twinkle.

"That is a likeness of a crocodile, not an alligator, Rudolph," she said. "And it has never been alive. It was made by an artisan in the Gold Coast. I brought it back from there."

"That must be in Illinois," Hildy Helen said. "I don't think it's in Indiana."

"It is in Africa," Aunt Gussie said. She marched over to the carved figure Rudy had knocked over and set it upright on the table, replacing the drum. "This is a ceremonial drum from the Ivory Coast," she said. "And the mask you are manhandling, Hildegarde, is made of cowry shells from the Belgian Congo. Both of those places are in Africa, as well.

"Now," Aunt Gussie said, dusting her hands together and facing Hildy Helen and Rudy. "I'm happy that you're both interested in my treasures, but until you learn how to handle them properly, you will have to obtain clearance from me to touch any of them. If you want to know about something, you only need to ask me. Perhaps your sadly neglected education can begin there." She led them through a wide archway.

Rudy sighed. There was a sword hanging on the wall that he would have liked to get his hands on before they went in to dinner.

"Hands off," Dad said, watching Rudy. "That's a Scottish backsword. You could cut someone's head off with that."

"How about Aunt Gussie's?" Rudy muttered.

Hildy Helen poked him in the rib. "Let's explore that big thing in the hall later," she whispered.

"What big thing?"

"I don't know what it is, but it looks like it opens. I bet we could get inside there!"

With that to look forward to, Rudy dragged his feet a little less as he passed through a parlor with a marble fireplace and a piano so long it made the one back at their church in Shelbyville look like a toy. He was about to stop and point out to Hildy Helen the statue of the naked man on a side table, but his father put his hand on his shoulder and steered him on. This was looking worse by the minute. With Aunt Gussie pointing out their every fault, his father was starting to correct them, something he almost never did.

I'm just going to have to set her straight, Rudy thought as he followed his great aunt into a sun-drenched dining room.

Dad hurried over to a straight-backed chair with arms at the head of the table and tried to help Aunt Gussie into it, but she swatted him away. She moved pretty well for an old lady, Rudy decided. He'd have to take that into consideration in any tricks he played on her.

The rest of them took their places at the round table. There were sideboards on every wall except the one that was filled with a bowed-out section of big windows, and every sideboard shelf was covered in expensive looking dishes.

There was a pitcher shaped like bamboo, a three-legged tray with a fierce looking warrior painted on it, and bronze candlesticks with feet like claws. There was every kind of saltcellar imaginable, including some shaped like dragons that Rudy would have loved to get his hands on, and vases of every description.

"Rudolph, we bow our heads when we ask the blessing in this house."

Rudy jerked his head to see Aunt Gussie narrowing her sharp eyes at him.

"Sure," he said. "Swell."

She sniffed. Rudy rolled his eyes at Hildy Helen before he closed them.

Dinner was delicious. At least, that was what Dad kept saying as he loaded his plate up again and again with lamb chops and French fried potatoes and peas. Rudy himself didn't taste much. It was hard to enjoy even a mouthful with Aunt Gussie watching his every move.

"Rudolph," she said, "keep your elbows off the table." And, "Hildegarde, a mouth is to be wiped with a napkin, not a sleeve." And, "Children, you see that rosewater ewer and basin in silver gilt over there on the sideboard? It was made in Germany before forks were invented so that diners who ate with their hands could wash between courses. You notice we don't use it now—we have forks!"

When she turned to Dad and said, "James, I have seen gorillas in the wild with better manners than these two," Rudy was ready to let fly with a forkful of peas, right between her beady little eyes. Hildy Helen had *her* eye on the Austrian vase in the middle of the table, which would have also made a good missile. By the time Quintonia put a piece of deep-dish apple pie with a chunk of cheese beside it in front of him, he wasn't hungry anymore. He was too busy planning what to do to show this Aunt Gussie person just who was in charge of Rudy Hutchinson's manners.

When Quintonia served the coffee with cream, Rudy said in as rough a voice as he could muster, "Dad, I don't drink coffee. Can I go now, please?"

"*May* I," Aunt Gussie said promptly.

"You don't need to go with us, Aunt Gussie," Hildy Helen said. "Stay and drink coffee with Dad."

"I was correcting his grammar, child," Aunt Gussie said.

"There ain't nothin' wrong with my grammar," Rudy said. Then he grinned and, without waiting for his father's nod, left the dining room.

"Let's play in that big case thing," Hildy Helen whispered from behind him.

But Rudy shook his head as he hurried through the parlor and into the big hall. "I'm goin' outside," he said. "I gotta find me a mouse."

"Mouse! Eek!" someone suddenly shrieked. "Mouse! Mouse! Eek! Eek!"

"Who was that?" Hildy Helen said.

"You got me," Rudy said. He craned his neck toward a doorway at the front of the hall. "I think it came from in there."

"It sounded like an old man."

"Old man? No, old woman!" Rudy stared at Hildy Helen in horror. "You don't think Aunt Gussie has a twin sister, do you?"

"Mouse!" the voice shrieked again. "Eek!"

Hildy Helen poked him in the rib. "Let's go look."

Rudy nodded and crept carefully toward the doorway. There was some low muttering, just like an old woman talking to herself. Half afraid he was going to see someone identical to Aunt Gussie, Rudy peeked around the corner.

"Eek! Mouse! Mouse!" the voice screamed—and Rudy jumped back with a scream of his own.

"Rudy!" Hildy Helen cried. "It's a bird! And it talked!"

✝ ⸎ ✝

Chapter Four

Hildy Helen was right. All that noise *was* coming out of a bird—and this was no worm-pulling robin. The thing had to be two feet tall and had such bright green and red feathers Rudy wasn't sure it hadn't been hand-painted like one of Aunt Gussie's artifacts.

The bird blinked, stared at them for a minute, and then commenced squawking again.

"Eek—mouse! Mouse!"

"Would you hush up?" Rudy hissed to it. "You're gonna give it away."

"Give it away. Give it away."

"Hush!"

"Give what away?" Hildy Helen said.

"I'm gonna get a mouse and put it in Aunt Gussie's bed tonight."

"In Aunt Gussie's bed. In Aunt Gussie's bed. Mouse! Eek!"

The twins both sprayed the bird with a *shh*! and it went back to muttering.

"Guess I can't play *that* trick," Rudy said.

Hildy Helen blinked at the bird, who blinked back at her. "This bird talks, Rudy," she said.

"Yeah, and too much if you ask me. You can't say anything around him or he blabs it all over."

"Blabs it all over! Blabs it all over!"

Rudy shook his head. "See what I mean?"

Hildy's eyes took on a gleam, and she leaned toward the gilt cage the big bird was perched in. "Can you say, 'Aunt Gussie is a meanie'?"

Obediently, the bird opened his giant beak and said, "Aunt Gussie is a meanie."

Hildy Helen giggled. Rudy grabbed her arm. "This is perfect!" he said. "We can show Aunt Gussie who she has to reckon with here."

"You think so?" Hildy Helen said.

"Sure! Next time she walks in here, she's going to get an earful of 'Aunt Gussie is a meanie! Aunt Gussie is a meanie!' "

"And what will that do?" Hildy Helen said. She always asked him 10 thousand questions about his plans.

"It'll let her know what we think of her, and maybe she'll leave us alone some."

"That *would* be nice," Hildy Helen said. "Have you ever gotten so many instructions in one meal in your life?"

Rudy skewed his voice up into a high squawk. "Use a napkin, not a sleeve."

"Not a sleeve. Not a sleeve," the bird said.

Hildy Helen and Rudy grinned at each other.

"You're right. This is perfect," Hildy said.

"But we can't have him say it when we're in the room," Rudy said.

"But I want to hear him say it to her. That's half the fun."

"Then we'll just have to hide."

Rudy looked around the new room they were in, which was obviously some kind of library. There was a desk at one end, a rectangular table in the center lined with chairs, and bookshelves from floor to ceiling on four sides of the room. Urns, jars, and lamps with bases shaped like Greek statues dotted every horizontal surface. The place was loaded with interesting clutter, but there were no good hiding places.

"Where's that big thing you were talking about?" Rudy said.

"You mean the big case?"

"Yeah."

"Out in the hall. Come on."

Hildy Helen hurried out. Rudy stopped beside the birdcage. "Aunt Gussie is a meanie," he said to the bird.

It cocked its head.

"When she comes in, just say that at her—scream it at her. You got it?"

"You got it? You got it?"

"No, say, 'Aunt Gussie is a meanie.' "

"Aunt Gussie is a meanie."

Rudy left it at that and went out into the hall, where Hildy Helen was proudly holding open the door to a case that was shaped like a body.

"I saw one of these on a movie poster," Rudy said. "It's some kind of Egyptian thing."

"There's room in here for both of us if we squish," Hildy Helen said. "Hurry up! I think I hear them coming!"

"Aunt Gussie is a meanie!" the bird squawked.

Stifling their giggles, the twins squeezed into the case and managed to pull the door shut. It had smelled like a doctor's office, and it made Rudy wrinkle his nose. But if this worked on Aunt Gussie, it would be worth sniffing a little bad odor.

Seconds later, Aunt Gussie's sensible pumps could be heard thumping across the floor with Dad's leather soles behind her.

"Don't fret about it, James," she was saying. "I have the situation well in hand. You turned out all right, didn't you?"

"There was only one of me," Dad said.

Their voices faded off into the study, and Rudy felt Hildy Helen squeeze his hand. That either meant she was excited, or she had to go to the bathroom, or both.

"Who's this?" they heard their father say.

"Aunt Gussie is a meanie! Aunt Gussie is a meanie!"

"What did it say? Did that bird talk?"

Aunt Gussie didn't answer. Her heels thumped their way out into the hallway, and inside the case, Rudy held his breath until he thought he'd explode.

"Aunt Gussie is a meanie! Aunt Gussie is a meanie!"

"I heard you, Picasso," Aunt Gussie said, her voice crackly-dry, "and I'm just about to prove you right. Rudolph! Hildegarde! Come here at once!"

Rudy could feel Hildy's shoulders shaking with laughter. He let out some air and gulped it in again before he could burst into giggles.

"Children! Now!"

"Now! Now!" Picasso echoed.

Rudy squeezed his eyes shut, but his laughter came out his nose and sprayed Hildy Helen's shoulder. She snuffled up a guffaw, but her shoulders were shaking out of control. And so, it seemed, was the case they were in.

"Oh, no!" Rudy hissed.

He put out his hands to steady its sides, but it was too late. As Hildy Helen kept trembling with giggles, the case began to sway forward, and it wouldn't stop.

"We're going down!" Rudy whispered.

And they did. They landed on the hallway floor with a heavy thud and let their laughter go. When the case was rolled over and the door opened, their screaming was even louder than Picasso's.

"Oh, my stars," Dad said. "Is it damaged, Auntie?"

"It's four thousand years old and was dumped on the floor by a couple of ruffians. What do you think?" Aunt Gussie thrust out her hands and yanked both twins up to their feet with surprising strength. They stood there, still trying to smother their laughter as Aunt Gussie and Dad righted the case and returned it to its place.

"Looks like just a few flakes of paint nicked off," Dad said. He tried to laugh. "They don't make them like this anymore, do they?"

"What is that thing, anyway?" Hildy Helen said.

"It's an ancient mummy case," Aunt Gussie said. "They buried dead bodies in those in Egypt."

Rudy sobered. "Was there ever a dead body in that one?"

"Yes, and there's likely to be again unless you two do precisely as I say. Into the parlor, both of you."

Rudy looked at his father, but he was busy cleaning his glasses with a handkerchief. Rudy couldn't read his face. Hildy Helen grabbed Rudy by the arm and tugged him along with her.

"Maybe we should just do what she says," Hildy Helen whispered. "I don't want to be a mummy."

After what Aunt Gussie told them in the parlor, however, Rudy wasn't so sure he agreed with Hildy Helen.

"Now then," their aunt said when she had them seated on a couch whose arms resembled a lion's paws, "it is obvious to me that you are uneducated, untrained, and completely uncivilized. I can't really blame your father for that. He's been trying to raise you alone all your lives and keep a law practice afloat as well. But that is all changed now that you're here in my charge."

"Your charge?" Rudy said. "What about our dad?"

He looked around the room, but Dad was nowhere in sight. Rudy had a sudden sinking feeling.

"Your father is going to be busy with his new endeavors," Aunt Gussie said. "And I shall be busy with mine, which will be to teach you enough manners so that you will not embarrass yourselves in public, and then make certain that you each learn some skill that will make you socially endearing."

"What does that mean?" Hildy Helen aksed. Her voice sounded hopeful. Rudy wasn't hoping for anything.

"That means something that will make you an asset to social gatherings," Aunt Gussie said. "Hildegarde, you will start with the piano. Lessons will begin tomorrow."

Rudy couldn't help but smirk. The thought of sturdy, mischievous Hildy Helen sitting prettily at that huge piano would make a good cartoon. He'd have to draw one tonight.

"As for you, Rudolph—" Aunt Gussie began.

Rudy straightened in spite of himself.

"You will begin with the violin."

Hildy Helen burst right out laughing.

"I see nothing humorous in that," Aunt Gussie said. "Learning a stringed instrument teaches self-discipline and self-control—both of which your brother is entirely lacking. Tomorrow afternoon, you will take bow in hand, my boy." She dusted her hands in that way she had whenever she was changing the subject. "Now, then, tomorrow *morning*, you will accompany me to Hull House, where you will learn about your obligations to society. Be ready immediately after breakfast, which is served at 8:00. Quintonia will wake you at 7:00 so you can bathe." She pulled her glasses down her nose and surveyed the twins over the tops of their wire rims.

By then it was growing dark, and Quintonia was summoned in to escort them up to their rooms on the second floor. Aunt Gussie's was on the first floor, it seemed, and Rudy muttered to Hildy Helen that their aunt should thank her lucky stars, or he'd have a spider or *something* in her bed so fast it would make the old lady's head spin.

Rudy barely looked at his own room as he stripped off his

clothes, dumped them in a corner, put on his pajamas, and climbed into the high bed with its headboard that reminded him of bars on a jail cell. He'd seen those on a Tom Mix poster, too.

But even thoughts of his favorite movie star didn't cheer him up. As he lay there watching the hot evening breeze puff the drapes out from the window, he could hear a train wailing its lonely whistle down a nearby track—and beyond that the faint horns and rattles and screeches of the big, scary city. His stomach started to churn once more—and Rudy Hutchinson didn't like it when his stomach churned and his heart hurt with homesickness. He didn't like it at all. Tomorrow, he was going to have to find a way to change that.

But before he was even fully awake the next morning, Rudy heard two things that perked him up, just a little.

One was the sound of a telephone ringing, and that brought him straight up in bed.

A phone! he thought. *Swell!*

His father had a telephone in his office back in Shelbyville, but he had never had one installed in their home. It wasn't because Rudy hadn't begged him. He'd thought a thousand times how much fun it would be to call people up and say things like, "Do you have Prince Albert in a can? If you do, please let him out!" It sounded like even more fun than knocking on old people's doors and then running away before they could get there.

Rudy got up and went out into the hall in his pajamas to see if he could figure out where the telephone was. He could hear Quintonia talking away on it, down in the room where Picasso was. The library, Aunt Gussie had called it. As he stood there, he heard the second sound—the static noise of a radio being tuned in.

That sent Rudy hauling right down the stairs and into the

library, where Quintonia was just placing the telephone receiver back onto its candlestick-shaped holder and fiddling with some knobs on a dark brown radio at the same time.

"This just in," a deep voice said from its speaker. "There has been another street shooting, this time killing mobster Baby Joe Esposito, known to be right-hand man to racketeer and bootlegger Big Tim Murphy, who was recently assassinated. The murder of Baby Joe Esposito occurred yesterday in front of Union Station. Police have called in gang leader Al Capone for questioning."

"What are we listening to?" Rudy said to Quintonia.

"The news, same as we do every morning," she said. "Miss Gussie, she like to know what's goin' on in Chicago."

"What comes on after the news?" Rudy said, settling himself in a chair. "*Cheerio*? I've heard about that show. Or *Fu Manchu*? That's on the *Collier Hour*, I think."

"Aunt Gussie don't listen to nothin' but the news," Quintonia said.

Rudy could feel his lip curling. "That's all?"

"That's all."

"She doesn't believe in all that hooey they believe in Shelbyville, does she?" Rudy said. "About the radio waves making people sick and all that? That isn't true, you know."

"Miss Gussie don't believe in no nonsense," Quintonia said indignantly. She put her big, bony hands on her hips and glared down at Rudy. "What she do believe in is people doin' they work and not fritterin' away they time listenin' to programs."

"I don't have any work to do," Rudy said.

"Oh, but you do."

Aunt Gussie's voice cracked from the doorway. Under a white

cover that was draped over his cage, Picasso stirred his feathers and squawked, "Oh, but you do! Oh, but you do!"

Rudy really wanted to tell that bird to shut his beak.

✛ ✛ ✛

Chapter Five

*F*eeling as if he were being poked with pins, Rudy took his bath in the big upstairs bathroom with its sink on a pedestal and its long bathtub on feet. Hildy Helen commented later that at least that room was modern, but Rudy wasn't impressed. In the car after breakfast, he sulked as Sol drove the Pierce Arrow toward the West Side.

"So, what is this Hull House place we're going to?" Hildy Helen said.

Why are you bothering to even ask her? Rudy thought sullenly. *All she's going to do is tell you it's bad manners or correct your grammar or something, the old meanie.*

Aunt Gussie sighed and shook her head. "You've not heard of Hull House, either?"

"Nope," Hildy Helen said.

"Miss Jane Addams founded Hull House for all the immigrants who came to America looking for a better life and found a pit of despair instead."

"What's an immigrant?" Hildy Helen asked.

"A person from a foreign country. An immigrant leaves his or her country for good and transplants here."

"Just like us coming from Indiana," Rudy mumbled.

"You could say that," Aunt Gussie said. "Only these poor people don't have the opportunities you two have. They don't speak English. They don't understand how we do things here in the United States. So Miss Jane Addams set up a settlement house where the immigrants on the West Side could learn how to live in the new country, maybe learn a trade, learn the language—anything they needed. She has 13 buildings now. It takes up a whole block on Halsted. I'd say there are 9,000 people going through there every week."

"But we aren't *really* immigrants," Hildy Helen said, sitting up straight on the leather seat. "Rudy was just joking. He does that a lot."

Aunt Gussie looked at her over the tops of her glasses. "Does he now?" she said. Then she chuckled to herself and shook her head. "You aren't going as immigrants, girl. You're going to work there."

Rudy could hardly keep himself from groaning. Just the thought of scrubbing floors was enough to make his hands break out in blisters.

"But I thought you were rich," Hildy Helen said. "Why do we have to work?"

"Work isn't just about money," Aunt Gussie said. "Don't get yourselves all mixed up in what wealth can buy. That's what's wrong with this country right now. Everyone is so busy getting rich, they aren't thinking anymore. It's all going to come crashing down on them, you mark my words." She shook her head again. "There are some who would call me a spoilsport."

"*Dad* is the spoilsport," Hildy Helen said. Her dark eyes clouded, and Rudy could see her setting her jaw.

"Why do you say that?" Aunt Gussie said.

"Because he won't let me get my hair bobbed."

Rudy covered his ears. He really didn't want to hear what Aunt Gussie had to say about *that*.

But to his surprise, she just said, "Hmmmm," and then leaned up to the front seat and shouted, "Sol, let us out in front, would you?"

"Yep," Sol said. "I do it every day."

"Because I tell you to every day," she said.

Even after Aunt Gussie's explanation, Rudy was still amazed when they turned onto Halsted Street and he saw Hull House—or Hull *Houses*. There *were* a lot of buildings, big brick ones with pointed roofs and fire escapes that zigzagged up their sides. And every one of them seemed to be swarming with people. There were dozens of boys his age dressed like he was, in knickers to their knees, high-topped shoes, and floppy caps with brims. There were women hauling babies and girls with big hair bows, dragging dolls. It was a lot like the rest of the city with all its crowding and bustling.

Or so Rudy thought until he got out of the car and got a closer look—and an even closer one when Aunt Gussie shooed them inside under a sign that read Butler Building. These people weren't like the white-faced businessmen he'd watched scurrying down the sidewalks yesterday. These people had dark faces, many of them. And some were wearing costumes like the band of gypsies that had come through Shelbyville last summer. Still others had jet black hair or talked fast in garbled sounding words. All of them looked different somehow. It made his stomach uneasy.

"Are we still in America?" he whispered to Hildy Helen with a grin.

She didn't have a chance to answer. Aunt Gussie turned to face them and said, "I will see you back here at noon for lunch. I shall be in the kindergarten room, back in the Mary Crane Building, but I do not expect to be disturbed."

"What are we supposed to do?" Hildy Helen said.

"Learn about Hull House," Aunt Gussie said. "And there will be no trouble."

"And there will be no trouble," Rudy said in a crackly voice when she was out of earshot.

"Learning about Hull House sounds easy enough," Hildy Helen said.

"But staying out of trouble doesn't." Rudy jammed his hands into the pockets of his knickers.

Hildy Helen sighed, too. "We haven't got anything else to do," she said. "We might as well explore. Who knows? Maybe you can find a way to trick Aunt Gussie here."

It was only that which got Rudy to follow his sister further into the depths of Hull House. After that, the house itself pulled him along.

It seemed every activity imaginable went on there. Amid the people busy with everything from play rehearsal to baseball practice, from adult pottery classes to children's painting workshops, there were craft shops, training kitchens, sewing rooms, and even a gymnasium. Rudy wanted to stay in the billiard room, and he was even more excited by the bowling alley. Hildy Helen was entranced by the dancing class and the club room, where a bunch of girls her age were voting on costumes for the Fourth of July parade.

The classrooms where people were learning English weren't as exciting, but the band room was teeming with activity—students banging on drums and blowing on horns and not sounding so awfully bad when Rudy thought about it. *That one instrument, that curved horn with all the keys, that would be fun to draw*, he thought. Rudy made a mental note to do a cartoon featuring one when they got back to Aunt Gussie's.

It was then that he realized he wasn't sulking anymore—that he was actually getting interested in what was going on here.

And that wouldn't do. That wouldn't do at all.

So at their next stop, he decided to get ahold of himself before Aunt Gussie thought she "had him well in hand." He followed

Hildy Helen into a crowded room, where a tangle of boys was gathered around a piano, which was being played by a white-haired lady with eyes like a bird.

"All right, boys!" she called out. "Remember my motto— 'Sing, and you'll be good.' "

"Yes, Miss Martha!" they shouted back at her.

"All right then!" she cried.

At once they burst into song, some of them chirping in trebly high-pitched voices, others croaking like toads who any minute might turn back into tadpoles if they didn't keep control over their vocal chords. But no matter how much they might have sounded like a toad-chorus, they were all grinning and clapping their arms around each other's shoulders and tapping their feet. It looked like fun.

But it was too perfect an opportunity to pass up. Rudy maneuvered himself behind Miss Martha and looked for a good target. He found one in the shortest boy in the group, a stocky kid with slicked-back dark hair who was singing for all he was worth, grabbing the front of his shirt with his hand and pointing his eyes to the ceiling and throwing his head around as if he were on center stage. Rudy waited until he caught the boy's eye.
he caught the boy's eye.

Then Rudy gave him a half-grin and opened his mouth, pretending to sing. He rolled his eyes up and clasped his chest and wagged his head. When he looked back at the boy, his eyes were hooded over with suspicion, and his mouth had closed down into a tight-lipped frown.

"Sing," Rudy mouthed to him, "and you'll be good."

The boy's face went blood-red, and he grabbed the shoulder of the boy in front of him as if he were going to climb right over him to get to Rudy. Rudy felt a hand clap over his own shoulder. It was Hildy Helen, yanking him out the door.

"What were you doing?" she said when she got him into the hall.

"Giving that kid the business," Rudy said. "Wasn't that the silliest thing you ever saw? I don't think he knew how silly he looked."

"He does now!"

They exchanged grins, which faded when Aunt Gussie sailed around the corner and said briskly, "Luncheon is served. Are your hands clean?"

"Luncheon" was another surprise. Rudy had somehow expected that they would eat in the mansion with Miss Jane Addams, since Aunt Gussie seemed so chummy with her. But instead, she ushered them into the residents' dining room and directed them to a long table, where a bunch of men and women with broad, flat brown faces were already sitting.

"At least here she can't bother us about our manners so much," Hildy Helen said under her breath.

And she didn't. In fact, their aunt was quite busy chattering away with everyone around her, in a language Rudy had never heard before.

"I like the way it sounds," Hildy Helen said.

Rudy found himself liking a lot of things, including the round loaves of golden bread, the peach cobbler, and the noodles all piled up in bowls and covered with red sauce. It was all served on heavy pottery plates with bright flowers painted on them. The man next to Rudy proudly motioned to him with his hands that he had made some of them.

Someone in a corner was playing a guitar, and as people finished their meals and cleared their dishes, they sang along. This time Rudy didn't mock anyone. He was having too much fun.

But the fun didn't last. Soon Aunt Gussie announced to them that it was time to leave, and she told Rudy to go signal Sol to bring the car up to the front. The minute he stepped out onto

Halsted Street, Rudy was suddenly on the ground, beneath a hot, smelly, wriggling mass of flying fists and kicking feet.

"Hey, let me go!" he cried out.

They didn't, of course. What seemed like a hundred boys picked him up and carried him like a sack of flour down the sidewalk and into an alley. With a thud, they dropped him to the ground and stood around him in a leering circle, while several of them fumbled at his clothes and turned his pockets inside out.

"He ain't got nuttin'!" one boy said.

"He's gotta have somethin'. He's a rich boy!" another one growled.

"I'm tellin' ya, he ain't got nuttin'. You callin' me a liar?"

"Yeah, I guess I am!"

There was a temporary scuffle as the boys turned on each other. Rudy took that opportunity to try to scramble up, but a foot planted firmly on his shoulder held him there.

These are all the choirboys, Rudy thought as he stared up at them and tried not to look as terrified as he felt. *How come they didn't seem so tough when they were all around the piano?*

One more boy patted him roughly with his hands and shook his head at the others. "He wasn't lyin'. This boy ain't got nuttin'."

"He's a waste of time," another one said.

That seemed to be the signal for everyone to give Rudy one last half-hearted kick and stroll off. All except the boy whose foot was still planted on Rudy's shoulder.

The boy was suddenly down on top of him, his nose an inch from Rudy's. He was the singer Rudy had mocked just a few hours ago.

"You like to make fun of people, don't ya?" he said.

"Who me?" Rudy said. He tried to grin.

The kid yanked him up by his shirt and shoved him against the alley wall. Rudy tried to breathe but couldn't. He could feel the boy's breath going right up his nose, though.

"You know who I am?" the boy said.

"No," Rudy said.

"I'm Alonzo Delgado, better known as Little Al."

"Good for you," Rudy said. He hoped "Little Al" couldn't hear his heart pounding inside his chest.

"It is good for me, but it's bad for you, if you don't watch your back," Little Al said. "Because I got connections with the Big Man himself."

"The Big Man," Rudy said. "Who's the Big Man?"

Little Al's black eyes went wide, and he pulled in his chin as if Rudy had just said, "Who's Tom Mix?"

"*The* Big Man—the Boss," Little Al said.

"Don't know him."

"Al Capone, ya moron! Everybody knows Al Capone!"

At that point, Rudy *was* feeling like a moron, and he wasn't used to that. Back home in Indiana, nobody would have done this to him. They all knew if you fooled with Rudy Hutchinson, he got you back with one of his pranks. Things were different here— much different.

"You're getting me now, aren't ya, buddy boy?" Little Al said.

"Sure," Rudy said. "Now would you let go of me before Sol comes looking for me?"

That sounded good, didn't it? This boy had his Al Capone. Rudy had his Sol.

"Sol?" Little Al said. "Never heard of him." He brushed it off with a toss of his head that didn't disturb even a strand of his slicked-back hair.

"Go run to Sol then," Little Al said. He stepped back and watched Rudy brush off his clothes. "But just remember who I am next time, you got it?"

"Yeah, sure," Rudy said. He tried to swagger as he walked off.

As soon as he turned the corner onto Halsted, though, he broke into a run.

He was so busy trying to get his stomach to stop doing flips, he didn't notice on the way back to Prairie Avenue how quiet Hildy Helen was being in the car. But when they got there and he said, "Wait 'til you hear what happened to me," she burst into tears and ran off through the hall and out the door that led to the courtyard behind Aunt Gussie's house. By the time he caught up with her, she was facedown on a bench, sobbing until her shoulders shook.

"Jeepers, Hildy Helen," he said, standing miserably over her. "What's wrong?"

"I'm never going to get to be modern!" she wailed.

"Huh?"

"Aunt Gussie is so old-fashioned and frumpy and stiff. I'm not going to learn anything about being modern like I hoped. And now I'll never be a flapper or get my hair bobbed or have a life of my own!"

He slumped down on the ground beside her. "You're probably right," he said.

"I know I'm right! Things couldn't be any worse—even if we went back to Shelbyville right now!"

He was about to agree with her. But just a few minutes later, things did get worse—much worse.

✛ ✛ ✛

Chapter Six

*H*ildegarde! Rudolph! It's time for your music lessons!"

The dry voice calling from the hallway door crackled right up Rudy's backbone.

"You see what I mean?" Hildy Helen said. "She calls me 'Hildegarde!'"

"Well, at least you don't have to take stupid violin lessons!"

"Oh, and you can picture me playing the piano?"

Her face was starting to crumple again, and Rudy shook his head hard until the curls flopped down onto his forehead. "Don't worry, I'll think of something."

"You'd better do it fast," Hildy said. "Because I feel a tantrum coming on."

"Chil-dren! Now!"

Hildy Helen's face fell into a pout as she stomped off toward the hall door. As he followed, Rudy got the wheels turning in his head—the ones that were famous for cranking out ways to drive teachers, nannies, and housemaids clean out of their minds.

At the door, Aunt Gussie pointed him toward the room at the bottom of the entrance stairs, one of the places he hadn't had a chance to explore yet.

It turned out to be a strange room, its windows up high to

44

reach street level. There were, of course, more artifacts: some gleaming andirons with eagle heads near the fireplace, an old sea trunk that looked as if it had been around the world several times and not treated too well on the way, and a tall case clock that appeared as stern as Aunt Gussie.

"You are Rudolph?" said a voice.

Rudy turned to see a small, olive-skinned man with his hair slicked back like Little Al's. Standing there with both arms behind his back, he looked at Rudy with large, soulful black eyes, and Rudy was certain the man was about to cry. Rudy decided to help him along in that direction.

"I don't know any Rudolph," Rudy said.

"Then who are you?"

Rudy grinned. "I'm Rudy. Who are you?"

The man mouthed the words Rudolph and Rudy before his face lit up and he nodded. "Ah, I see! I am Leonardo Puchiarello!"

He said it with a great deal of trilling of the tongue, and Rudy had to snort to keep from laughing. Immediately, Leonardo's face went dark.

"Why do you laugh?" he said. He was talking strangely, Rudy thought, as if he were trying to have an accent.

"Why doesn't anybody around here have a normal name?" Rudy said. "Puchiarello?"

"It is Italian!" Leonardo cried, flailing the violin and bow above his head. "I am proud of it, as you should be of your name!"

"What's so swell about Hutchinson?"

"Rudolph, Rudolph! I am not a Hutchinson, but even I am proud to be a part of a family that has been teaching violin to the Hutchinsons for generations. Your father was given instruction in this very room by *my* own father."

"My father played the violin?" Rudy said.

Leonardo nodded, his eyes closed. Rudy spewed out a laugh that left little droplets on Leonardo's cheek.

Leonardo whipped a handkerchief from his pocket, mopped his cheek, and then thrust the hanky toward Rudy.

"I don't need it, thanks," Rudy said.

"Yes, you do. Put it under your chin."

"Why?"

"Because that is where the violin is going to go."

"No, see, you don't understand," Rudy said. "Maybe Aunt Gussie could make my father play this *thing*, but I'm not—"

Leonardo shoved the handkerchief into Rudy's neck, poked the violin on top of it, and smacked the bow into Rudy's hand.

"You're gonna play this thing, kid. Your Aunt Gussie's the toughest doll I know and she don't take no for an answer, so you might as well get started, y'hear?"

Rudy stared at Leonardo's suddenly hardened face and watched it slowly melt back to its big-eyed wonder.

"Now, then," he said, the accent firmly back in place. "Let us begin."

For an hour Rudy made scratching, screeching, blood-curdling noises on the strings until his neck had a crick in it and he knew his face was pruned up. When Leonardo finally said, "That should do for today, Rudolph," Rudy tossed the violin to him and bolted from the room shouting, "Hildy Helen! Where are you?"

"What you doin', yelling like that inside this house?" Quintonia said. She was standing in the hallway with a feather duster, tickling the face of what appeared to be someone's head, shrunken down to the size of a melon.

"I'm looking for Hildy Helen."

"Well, everybody on the South Side know that, the way you shoutin'."

"Have you seen her?"

"Mmm-hmm."

Rudy waited, but Quintonia kept dusting.

Rudy shifted his feet. "Well, are you gonna tell me where?"

"Mmm-hmm."

Rudy waited again and forced himself not to stomp. "Well, *when* are you gonna tell me?"

"Soon's you ask polite."

"Oh."

She really was maddening enough to make a person pop a blood vessel, but she did it with such a calm, cool expression on her face.

"Miss Quintonia, if you please," he said, giving her a stiff bow, "I should like to know where I might find Miss Hildegarde. Do you happen to know?"

"I happens to know she's out yonder in the courtyard," Quintonia said. "And don't you slam that door on your way out, or I'm gonna have me some boy backside."

"Certainly," Rudy said. He bowed again and walked sedately to the door. Once he was outside, though, he tore across the courtyard that ran all the way alongside the house, closed in by high brick walls on three sides and the house itself on the other. Hildy Helen was pacing up and down on the grass like a madwoman.

"Hildy Helen," he said when he got to her, "that was the stupidest thing in the *world!*"

"You're telling me," she said. "I had to make 'little bear paws' with my hands for an hour. Look at this! I think I'm crippled for life!"

She held out her hands like a pair of claws, but Rudy only gave them a glance.

"That's it," he said. "We have to talk Dad into taking us back to Indiana."

"That's just what I was going to say."

He started to take off, but she grabbed his sleeve. "Do you even know where his office is?" she said.

"No."

"And if we did, how would we get there? This isn't like running across the street in Shelbyville."

"All right, then tonight we'll get to him the minute he walks in the door."

"And then he's going to say that we haven't given it a chance."

"One day's long enough for me!" Rudy said.

"Well, me, too. But it isn't going to be long enough for him. I think we should wait a couple of days and then talk to him."

"I can't stand it for a couple of days!"

"Rudy!" she said. "Have you actually found someone you can't trick?"

Rudy started to nod, but he didn't. "All right," he said, shrugging. "I guess it won't kill me."

But over the next three days, he wasn't quite sure he wouldn't die any minute. Every time they sat down at a meal, Aunt Gussie was like a frog, lashing her tongue out at their manners and their grammar as if they were flies. Elbows, napkins, and proper forks were the main topics of conversation. Rudy looked more than once at his father for a rescue, if he were actually there at the table, but Dad would only follow one of Aunt Gussie's tirades about Rudy talking with his mouth full with a question like, "Auntie, what do you know about these bomb threats?"

Neither Rudy nor Hildy Helen could walk through the house without Quintonia appearing with feather duster in hand, telling them to pick up their feet and their dirty clothes and to keep their hands *off* everything else, including Picasso.

"You touch that bird and you liable to draw back a nub," she told them one day when they were poking their fingers into the cage.

"He bites?" Hildy Helen said.

"No, but Miss Gussie does," Quintonia said.

The worst was every afternoon when Rudy screeched away with Leonardo, who shouted instructions that made no sense.

After every lesson, Aunt Gussie would usher the twins into the library to "get acquainted" with the books that lined the walls. Hildy Helen would take a few down and half-heartedly look at the pictures, but Rudy refused to do even that much. He did find some paper in a drawer, however, and spent his time drawing cartoons of Aunt Gussie featuring large, evil-looking teeth and beady little hawk eyes behind glasses.

"You better hope she never sees those," Hildy Helen said. "Or she's liable to put *you* in a cage."

"I'm already in one," he said.

It sure felt like it, anyway. They rarely saw their father, who was busy setting up his new office, and they seldom heard the radio unless it was tuned to some boring show Aunt Gussie was listening to about the stock market or the mayor.

The only time Aunt Gussie did loosen the reins was in the mornings when they went to Hull House. In spite of her saying that they were "working," she dismissed them at the door when they arrived and told them not to bother her until lunch. They were free to do whatever they wanted.

One day they helped some men build a fence around a baseball field in an empty lot next door. On another they watched some Mexican pottery students throw pots, and one of them let Rudy turn the wheel. Rudy only stuck one wad of clay in Hildy Helen's ear.

They tasted fruit cobbler in the training kitchen and did exercises with some kids in bloomers in the gymnasium and watched a boy cane a chair. Rudy made it a point to stay away from Miss Martha's singing class or anyplace else where Little Al and his friends went. It made his stomach churn one day when he saw them building a clubhouse made from things they were dragging from the very alley where they'd thrown Rudy on the ground. What they were doing looked like fun, but for the first time in his life, Rudy was afraid of somebody.

Little Al found ways to make it clear that Rudy *ought* to be quaking in his high-tops. No matter how hard he tried to avoid Al, Rudy seemed to run into the kid at every turn. The day in the gym was only one example.

Rudy was watching a boxer train when suddenly Little Al was beside him, saying, "Ya see that bag he's punchin'?"

"Yeah," Rudy said.

"Just think of that as your head if you don't watch your back."

"Gee, Alonzo," Rudy said, "you sure know how to make a guy feel at home." But inside, his heart was thundering.

"He thinks he's a smart guy," one of Little Al's friend muttered. "I'd punch him just for that."

"Nah," Rudy said. "Wait 'til I do something bigger."

They all poked each other and gave each other knowing looks, as if they were aware of some secret Rudy didn't know about. He smirked at them, in spite of his churning stomach and the lonely, left-out feeling in his chest.

That was the day he was pretty sure he *was* going to die if he didn't get back to Shelbyville, where he knew who he was and where he stood. Hildy Helen was feeling it, too, and that night, when Dad finally dragged in long after they'd had their supper, they sat on either side of him in the dining room while he ate leftover pot roast and blurted it all out.

"Aunt Gussie's mean!"

"I hate the violin!"

"Quintonia won't even let us breathe!"

"We never have time to play!"

"Aunt Gussie hates us. She even hates the way we talk!"

"I'm sick of wiping my mouth with my napkin every minute!"

"Please, Dad, send us back to Shelbyville."

"We won't drive our nanny crazy. We promise we'll be good!"

At that, their father pushed his plate away and looked from one to the other. His small eyes were popping behind his glasses, and his mouth was halfway open.

"I'm astonished!" he said.

"We knew you would be," Hildy Helen said. "We know how much you love Aunt Gussie, and we knew this would break your heart."

"I'm not brokenhearted, I'm flabbergasted. I can't believe you don't love it here!"

"Love it?" Rudy said. "I hate it!"

"Haven't you been listening, Dad?" Hildy Helen said, her arms folded across her chest. "Aunt Gussie is—well, she's a beast!"

Dad threw back his head and laughed so hard, he had to take off his glasses and wipe his eyes.

"Don't use your sleeve, James," Rudy said in a crackly voice. "That's what you have a handkerchief for."

Dad shook his head, still grinning—a sight they didn't see often. "You two have been bamboozled!" he said.

"What's 'bamboozled'?" Hildy Helen said.

"He means fooled," Rudy said. "I haven't been fooled, Dad."

"Ah, but you have. Give it time, you two. Aunt Gussie has to find you before she'll let you see who she really is."

"What do you mean 'find us?' " Hildy Helen said. "We're right here!"

"And I don't *want* to be right here!" Rudy said.

Dad stretched out his arms and scooped them both into his chest and rubbed their heads. "But right here is where you are and where you'll stay," he said. "And don't worry—it will all come out in the wash."

Rudy wriggled away and escaped to his room, where he flopped down in the middle of the big jail-bed and scratched out a sketch of Aunt Gussie on her hands and knees, looking under a tablecloth for Rudy and Hildy Helen. Then he crumpled it into a ball and hurled it across the room. It narrowly missed hitting Hildy Helen head-on as she came in the door.

"Sorry," Rudy said.

"I've been throwing things, too," she said. She climbed up onto the bed beside him. "What are we going to do?" she said. "Dad says give it time."

"But we don't *have* time," Rudy said. He shook his head. "No, I'll tell you what we're going to do. We're going to make it so miserable for Aunt Gussie having us here, she's going to *make* us leave."

"We'd better do it before she 'finds' us, whatever that means."

"It's just gobbledygook," Rudy said.

But long after Hildy Helen had gone off to her own room, Rudy lay watching the curtains listlessly blow.

Aunt Gussie will never find me, he told himself. *Because I'm way too lost here.*

✛ ✛ ✛

Chapter Seven

*R*udy started the next morning with a tried-and-true trick. He got to the dining room before anyone else came in for breakfast and sprinkled some itching powder in Aunt Gussie's napkin. It was hard to keep back an all-out guffaw as he thought about what the old lady was going to look like when that mouth she was always dabbing at during meals started twitching like a dying fly. He'd never known the itching powder to fail yet.

Until Aunt Gussie.

She sat herself crisply down at her place as usual, whipped the napkin off the table, and then shook it out as if she'd been forewarned that there was a snake inside. Rudy watched in dismay as powder flew up like dust in the sunlight streaming through the windows.

"Napkins in your laps, children," she said. She cut her eyes over the tops of her glasses at Rudy. "There will be no need for you to shake yours out, though, I'm sure. Mine was special."

And then she ate her poached eggs so neatly, she didn't have to dab her mouth even once.

"Do you think she knew it was there?" Hildy Helen whispered to him as they hurried toward the stairs after breakfast.

"I don't know," Rudy said. "But it doesn't matter. Wait 'til she

53

gets home this afternoon and finds out her goldfish are missing."

"Where are they going to be?" Hildy asked.

Rudy grinned and patted his stomach.

"No, you're really going to swallow them? Like those boys at the college we heard about?"

"Yep. I've been waiting for a chance to try it."

"Brush your teeth!" Aunt Gussie called from the direction of the living room.

"Yes, Aunt Gussie!" Rudy called back in his best good-boy voice. "Brush loud enough for both of us!" he hissed to Hildy Helen.

While she ran on up the stairs, Rudy crept into the library and made his way around the stacks of books and the globes on stands to the goldfish bowl on the table under the window. Three orange fish swam in mindless circles, and Rudy snickered down at them.

"Take one last lap, fishies," he said. "And then prepare to be dessert!"

Slowly he dipped his hand into the water and scooped up a tiny bundle of gold scales. The little fish flopped in his palm, and he had to cup his other hand over it to keep it from jumping right off onto the floor.

"I'll just slurp you right up," Rudy promised.

"Prepare to be dessert! I'll just slurp you right in! Slurp you right in!"

Rudy was the one to jump as Picasso screamed happily from his cage. The little gilt door was open, and the bird sat rocking in his "doorway."

"Picasso!" cried still another voice from the hallway. "Are you stalking those fish?"

In the second that he was startled by Picasso, Rudy's hands came open, and the fish took that opportunity to slither out and disappear somewhere on the rug. Rudy made a dive for the floor and peered under the table.

"Here, fishy!" he whispered. "I'll put you back in the bowl, I promise!"

"Back in the bowl! Back in the bowl!"

"Picasso! What are you babbling about?"

"Fishy! Fishy! Back in the bowl! Awk!"

His heart pounding, Rudy scooted under the table, nearly planting his knee right on top of the fish, whose miniature gills were gaping for water. Rudy snatched it up by the tail and opened his mouth. The tablecloth suddenly flew up in front of him and he found himself staring into Aunt Gussie's eyes. She didn't look terribly surprised.

"I found it, Aunt Gussie," he said, smiling sweetly. "Picasso must have dropped him under here when I found him dipping his beak into the fishbowl." He furrowed his brow at the fish. "I hope the poor little fella is still alive."

"Go ahead and swallow it, Rudolph," she said. "Ever since I heard about that ridiculous trend I've wondered how long a fish will actually live inside a human being's stomach."

She waited, while Rudy stared at the goldfish. "Live? Inside?" he said.

"Well, yes. Your insides are composed largely of water, so why wouldn't it live? Of course, when it gets hungry, it has to eat. But there is always the lining of your intestines to feast on, I suppose."

Rudy gulped and stuck out the fish to her. "I think he'll do better in the bowl."

"Oh," Aunt Gussie said. "Well, I suppose I shall have to run that experiment myself. Perhaps tonight at dinner. You haven't brushed your teeth. Get to it."

The rest of the day it was the same. Rudy was foiled at every turn. When he tried to let the air out of the tires on the Pierce

Arrow, Sol assumed he wanted to learn how to change a tire and had him groveling around on the ground for a good 30 minutes.

When the iceman—whom he'd heard Quintonia complain would tell all your family business to the whole city of Chicago if you gave him any information—came around that afternoon to fill their icebox, Rudy made it a point to be hanging around the kitchen porch when he came out and strike up a conversation. He told Iceman Ike that Aunt Gussie would need plenty of ice, because she'd taken to serving live fish for dinner. The old lady, he commented, probably ought to be locked up, crazy as she was.

Ike nodded sagely, and Rudy thought he finally had it. But then Ike took off his cap, smeared the sweat off of his forehead with his sleeve, and said, "I heard they already tried to commit her, and she done drove them people in the *asylum* crazy. Harriet Glowdowski, she told me that. Now you want to hear about a strange woman, that's Harriet. Do you know that—"

He kept Rudy on the porch for a good 45 minutes, until Rudy was so bored he would rather have spent the time with Aunt Gussie herself.

But he didn't see how his final plan could fail. He was headed into the library to teach Picasso some choice slang phrases that were guaranteed to knock the spectacles right off Aunt Gussie's nose, when Quintonia suddenly appeared out of the shadows of the hallway. She was as mean as Little Al. She was everywhere he was.

"What you doin'?" she said, setting the dust mop against the wall and putting her big bony hands on her hips. "You 'bout to get yourself into some mischief?"

"Who me?"

"That's who I'm talkin' to. I *know* you ain't goin' into that library to look at no books."

Rudy purposely widened his eyes. "Why wouldn't I take

advantage of the opportunities my Aunt Gustavia has given me to expand my—"

"Oh, hush up, boy. You got more baloney than the butcher. And don't you think for a minute everybody in this house don't know it, except for your daddy. And he got more important things to do than to worry 'bout you."

She shook her head and, to his surprise, picked up the mop again and went off chasing dust bunnies from under tables and chairs. Grinning, Rudy went into the library and up to Picasso's cage. The bird blinked at him and flicked a feather or two. Rudy blinked back.

Picasso was wearing a sign around his neck. "No Slang Spoken Here," it said.

"That's it," Rudy said to the bird. "I didn't want to do it, but I'm going to have to pull something big."

"Like what?"

Rudy jumped, but it was only Hildy Helen. This place and these people were getting to *him* instead of the other way around.

"You remember when we saw those college kids, the ones from University of Indiana that had the car?" Rudy said.

"With the sayings painted all over it?" she said. " 'Stop Me If You've Heard This' and 'Harvard Loves Princeton' and all that?"

"Yeah."

Hildy Helen shook her head until the hair parted over her ears. "No, Rudy," she said. "That's too much, even for you. Aunt Gussie wouldn't just send you home for painting on her car. She'd cut off your fingers or something!"

Picasso squawked and hid his face under his wing.

"See," Hildy Helen said. "He believes it, too."

"Then what?" Rudy said. "So far everything I've tried has fallen through. I think these walls have eyes and ears."

"Then do something away from here, like at Hull House."

Rudy felt his eyes take on a gleam. "Of course! Embarrass her in front of all those other old ladies who think she's doing good deeds. You know, the ones that all look like her? Got any ideas? What else do the college kids do?"

"Well, you could—"

"No, wait, I've got it!"

"What?"

Rudy started to open his mouth, but he could feel Picasso leaning in on his perch. Rudy cupped his hands around Hildy Helen's ear and whispered to her. When she pulled her face away, she was round-eyed. "No, Rudy, that's too dangerous," she said.

"No, it's not. Shipwreck Kelly did it for 23 days and seven hours."

"But he had people there to keep him awake so he wouldn't fall off."

"I won't have to stay there that long. As soon as Aunt Gussie sees me, she'll have me dragged down. And we'll be on the next train back to Shelbyville, I promise you."

"Do you swear?" she said.

"I swear."

The time until they went to Hull House the next morning dragged. Rudy must have told Hildy Helen a dozen times not to tell Aunt Gussie where he was, no matter how upset she got when she discovered him missing. "I want her to go crazy until she looks up and sees me for herself. Your job is to make sure she doesn't spot me until I get up there." The 13th time he reminded her, Hildy Helen said she was going to tell on him right now if he didn't quit nagging her.

The next day, Friday, Aunt Gussie bustled off to her kindergarten room as usual, and Rudy gave a sigh of relief. He was beginning to think she could read his mind and would decide to spend the day in the courtyard or something.

Once she was gone and Hildy Helen had gone to stand guard, Rudy wiped his hands on the back of his knickers, grabbed on to the flagpole, and shinnied his way to the top.

The view of Halsted Street was perfect. He could see all the shops he hadn't had a chance to explore yet—a bakery with enormous wedding cakes in its showcase, a bread shop that had loaves piled almost to the top of its window, and a grocery with bins of apples and oranges outside, practically inviting a 10-year-old boy to snatch one or two.

And by the time he'd sat there an hour, and then two, and then three, he was wishing he had one of those apples, or even a carrot, which he hated.

He shifted uncomfortably on the big ball at the top of the flagpole. *How did Shipwreck do this for 23 days?* he thought. *My backside is already bruised.*

But the sound of the noon whistle blaring from a nearby factory was reassuring. It was time for lunch, and soon after that, Aunt Gussie would be emerging from Hull House, hopefully with some of her lady friends in tow, and the search for Rudy would begin.

The hour crawled by as Rudy resituated himself on the ball for the hundredth time and retwisted his legs around the pole to hold on. Finally, the front doors came open and people began to stream from the building. The Pierce Arrow pulled up right below him with Sol at the wheel, and Rudy began to feel that thrill-up-the-backbone he always got when someone was about to find out she'd been given the business by Rudy Hutchinson. Or in this case, Rudolph.

Rudy didn't care what she called him now, as long as she called him a taxi to get to the train station. He even forgot how uncomfortable he was as he held on to the pole and craned his neck to watch the door.

He didn't have to wait long. Hildy Helen danced out, followed by the always straight-shouldered Aunt Gussie.

Don't tell her I'm up here, Rudy wanted to call to Hildy Helen just one more time. She herself was shading her eyes and looking right up at him, but Aunt Gussie headed straight for the car with her gray hat pulled down low over her forehead. She looked neither right nor left as Sol opened the door for her and she slipped inside the Pierce Arrow.

Hildy Helen stopped on the sidewalk, put her hands on her hips, and looked up at Rudy. His mind raced for a moment, but he shook his head at her and put his finger up to his lips.

The old lady's slipping, he thought. *She still hasn't figured out I'm not there. The minute she does, she'll be out of that car like somebody put a frog down her dress*.

Wishing he'd thought of *that* idea sooner, Rudy watched Hildy Helen get slowly into the car and look back up at him three times. But even as Sol started up the engine, the spoked wheels began to turn, and Hildy Helen stared at him in horror out the back window, Rudy just kept shaking his head and putting his finger up to his lips. Any minute now, just any minute now, Aunt Gussie would miss him and Sol would have to make a U-turn in the middle of Halsted Street.

But Sol left Halsted far behind him as he pulled away from the curb and disappeared into the traffic. Rudy sat stunned on the pole.

And there he sat all afternoon, as the brutal Chicago heat and its soaking humidity blistered his face and drenched it in sweat. By the time the sun finally started to dip behind Hull House, his tailbone felt as if it were about to split, and he was starving. But his stomach was churning as much with fear as with hunger, for two reasons.

One, he'd discovered this wasn't the best of neighborhoods. In the hours he'd sat on the pole, he'd witnessed three fistfights, two robberies of fruit stands, and several clumps of boys hiding in alleys smoking cigarettes and generally looking threatening.

Two, when he decided maybe he ought to just get down and

start walking back to Prairie Avenue, he discovered he couldn't. He couldn't make himself move to get into position to slide back down the pole, which he was sure had grown another 10 feet since he'd shinnied up it that morning. One move, he knew, and he'd go toppling to the ground so very, very far below him.

It was time for an emergency prayer.

Squeezing his eyes shut, he prayed: *God, I'm in trouble again. And this time I promise, if you'll just get me down, I'll just go back to Aunt Gussie's and do everything she says. I'll even learn to play the violin. But please, God, please just—*

The last word—the *help*—slipped out between his lips in a feeble yelp.

"Well," said a voice below him.

Rudy looked down into the shadows that were gathering in the courtyard. He still couldn't see anyone, but he heard the familiar voice again.

"I was wondering how long it was gonna take ya to start cryin'," the voice said. And out of the dimness stepped Little Al.

✠ ⁕ ✠

Chapter Eight

*I*f Rudy had been afraid before, he was sweating bullets now.

But I can't show it, he told himself as he waved casually down at Little Al. *Or I'm really in for it.*

Rudy cleared his throat. "What did you say? I'm so far up it's hard to hear up here."

"You heard what I said." Little Al put his thumbs in his suspenders and rocked back on his heels. "So why don't you get down?"

"You should see the view from up here. Why would I want to get down?"

"Because yer scared outta yer mind," Little Al said. "I been watchin' you. You ain't moved a muscle since lunch."

"I'm concentrating—which is hard to do with you jawin' down there, so do you think you could move on?"

"Then who's gonna get you down?"

"Who said I needed anybody to get me down?" *Somebody please get me down. God, please, let there be somebody—*

"You did," Little Al said. "I heard you say 'help.'"

"Nah, you're hearin' things. I can get down whenever I want to."

"So do it."

"I said whenever I want to. I don't want to."

Little Al shrugged. "When you change your mind, just holler out real loud. I'll be over at Geis's gettin' a pastry."

Rudy's stomach turned over as he watched Little Al start to move away.

"You want anything?" Little Al said. "Prune Danish? Cream puff? Some of them sandwiches with the cream cheese?"

Rudy couldn't help himself. He let out a whimper.

Little Al smiled. It wasn't much of a smile. He didn't move his mouth any more in a grin than he did when he talked. Rudy was sure he'd never seen anything that tough.

"Yer yella," Little Al said with a hard little laugh. "I knew it."

"No," Rudy managed to get out, "I think of myself as more blue. You know, a nice navy with maybe some white stripes—"

"Aw, shut yer yap and sit tight," Little Al said. "I'm comin' up."

Rudy clung to the pole and watched as the stocky boy made his way expertly upward until he was within feet of Rudy.

"When I get right below you, I'm gonna turn around," Al said. "Then you just slide down onto my back and hang on."

"Yeah, and then you'll dump me off and watch me fall on my head and die!"

"And miss the fun of havin' you kiss my feet when we get to the bottom? Huh!"

Little Al was still grunting out short, hard laughs as he maneuvered himself up to Rudy and turned around so that his shoulders were just right for grabbing on to.

"All right, I'll let you carry me down," Rudy said. "Just so you can look good to your friends. But I'm not kissing your feet."

"We'll see what my friends have to say about that."

Rudy didn't let that stop him from climbing onto Little Al's back and hanging on like a baby koala as the Italian kid slid back down the pole. He leaped off when they reached the bottom and held himself back from kissing the *ground*. He'd begun to think he'd never touch it again.

"Come on, pucker up," Little Al said. He threw back his slicked-up head and laughed.

Rudy looked around for the pack of dark-faced boys who seemed to follow Al like a cloud of dust, but they were nowhere in sight. They were probably back in the alley smoking.

Little Al lowered his face from his final laugh and looked surprised. "So, ain't you gonna run?" he said.

Rudy shrugged. "Nope," he said.

"Huh," Little Al said. "Maybe you ain't as yellow as I thought."

The truth was, it was almost dark, and although Rudy wanted to hightail it out of there, he had no idea how to get home or whether he could even make it that far, stiff and hungry as he was. But whatever his reason for staying, it seemed to impress Little Al.

"So maybe I got you figured all wrong," Al said. "You wanna hang around with me a while, maybe steal a few cigarettes, have a smoke in the alley? Hey, you hungry? We could hit my uncle up for some cannelloni."

The smoke didn't sound good but the food did, whatever cannelloni was. Rudy knew one thing for sure. Aunt Gussie wasn't coming back. If he was going to live through this, he was going to have to find his own way back to Prairie Avenue.

"Thanks for asking," Rudy said, "but I gotta get home."

Little Al nodded knowingly. "I get you. If I had your old lady for an old lady, I'd get home, too. She's one tough doll."

"I'm not scared of her," Rudy said.

Little Al rolled his eyes.

"So, look," Rudy said, "you know how I can get back to Prairie Avenue? I'm new around here."

Little Al's chest puffed out. "Sure. You got any money?"

"No." Rudy shifted uneasily on his feet. "Do I need some?"

"Nah, I got ways. Come on, only—"

He stopped and surveyed Rudy closely. Rudy looked down at his clothes and then back up at Little Al.

"What's wrong?" he said.

"If you're gonna hang around here," Al said, "you're gonna have to look a little tougher. Them curls hangin' down, they make you look like a sissy."

"I hate these," Rudy said. "I'm thinkin' of cuttin' 'em all off."

"Sure. Just stick 'em back under your hat—there—like that, see? Now get yer hands in yer pockets like so, and kinda throw your shoulders back when you walk. Well, that ain't it exactly, but it's close enough."

Little Al began to swagger off. Rudy followed, doing his best imitation.

"It's 'cause you ain't Italian that it don't come natural to ya," Little Al said. "But keep practicin'."

Rudy "practiced" for several blocks and was convinced they were going to walk all the way to the South Side, when suddenly Al whistled sharply through his teeth and a taxi cab pulled up beside them.

"I told you, I don't have any money," Rudy said nervously.

"Don't need none," Little Al. "Driver's my uncle."

They both slid into the backseat, and Rudy nodded to a curly-haired man, whose big barrel chest took up most of the front seat of his cab.

Little Al jabbered something to him in Italian, and the cab screeched away from the curb and wheeled off down the street. Rudy had barely gotten settled back in his seat when the cab stopped.

"That didn't get us very far," Rudy said.

"Got us to the eats," Al said.

He jerked a nod again, and Rudy found that they were standing in front of a small grocery store with a green and white awning that stretched out over the usual bins of vegetables and fruit. This one was also stocked with baskets of golden bread, sticking up in loaves the shape of baseball bats.

"Help yourself," Little Al said and grabbed an apple, which he rubbed against his pant leg and inspected for shine.

Rudy looked around warily. "What if we get caught?"

"By who?" Al said. "This is my uncle's store. He won't care."

Rudy selected an apple. "Do you have an uncle on every corner?" he said.

"Yeah, the only thing I don't got is a father. But who needs one, right?"

"Yeah, right," Rudy said. The bread turned to sawdust in his mouth. *I'm probably about to find out what it's like not to have a father,* he thought. *Mine's probably gonna throw me out when I get home.*

"Eat up," Little Al said. "We might have to fight our way down the street."

"I thought you were the tough guy in the neighborhood," Rudy said.

"In *my* neighborhood," Little Al said, puffing out his chest again. "But to get you home, we gotta go through Greektown, see? And they got a gang of boys that would make your hair curl. 'Course, yours is already curled. Get that back under yer hat, would ya? They'll kill ya for sure, if they see that."

Rudy's stomach turned completely inside out as he smashed his hair up under his hat and followed Little Al down the street. He didn't even try to copy Al's swagger this time. Rudy was scared to death.

And, it turned out, with good reason. They hadn't gone three blocks into Greektown when their path was suddenly blocked by a line of boys older than they were with faces that shone in the dark. Little Al shoved his sleeves up to his elbows.

"Look at the little wop!" one of the boys said. "He thinks he's gonna fight us!"

Yeah, Rudy thought. *Somebody stop him!*

But it looked as though nothing would stop Little Al. He stepped up to the Greek boy in the center of the line, puffed out his chest, and said, "Which one of ya's gonna be first?"

"First for what?" the boy said, lifting his upper lip in a white-toothed sneer.

"First for me to work you over if you don't get out of my way."

There was a harsh wave of laughter, and the whole line of them stepped forward as one. Little Al still stood there with his chest out, but Rudy's stomach lurched.

"I'm warning you guys. You better just go chase yourselves," Rudy said. "He may look like a puny, little Milquetoast, but he's a live wire, I'm tellin' ya. You know those Eye-talians. They got tricks."

Little Al looked at him, his eyes gleaming, and gave his tight, little smile. "Yeah—learned 'em all from the Boss himself."

Rudy leaned forward and whispered loudly, "That's Al Capone, case you didn't know."

The line stared for a half second before the tall boy in the center glinted his eyes at Little Al. "Yer just beatin' yer gums," he said. "You ain't nothin' but a bohunk."

"And what are you, the crown prince and his court?" Rudy said.

"I might be," the Greek kid said.

"Prove it," Rudy said.

Where he was going with that, he had no idea—and didn't have to. When the tall shiny-faced boy stepped forward, and the rest of his line with him, Little Al flung out an arm, took Rudy down at the knees, and himself scrambled between the feet of half a dozen of them. Rudy was right on his tail, getting his hands stepped on, but pulling out on the other side and taking off at a run after Little Al before he had even straightened up.

The Greek boys followed them in confusion for half a block until Little Al led Rudy down an alley, up a fire escape, and down onto a low roof which they jumped off and landed onto the top of a delivery truck. Little Al slid to the ground and put a hand up for Rudy, but he declined it and slid down himself. He was grinning as he got up off the dirt and dusted off his knickers.

"That was a swell trick!" Rudy said. "I'm gonna have to use that—"

"Sooner than you think if you don't stop beating up the chops and come on!"

Little Al took off down the dark street with Rudy right behind him.

"What's 'beating up the chops'?" he called out.

"Beatin' your gums—talkin' too much!"

"Oh, what's a 'bohunk'?"

"Immigrant, which I ain't," Al threw back over his shoulder. "Yer Eye-talian."

"It ain't 'Eye' talian. It's 'I' talian."

"Oh."

"And I ain't no puny little piece of toast, or whatever that was you said I looked like."

"Milquetoast," Rudy said. He doubled his pace to keep up with Little Al as they darted across a street full of honking cars in the middle of the block. "You never heard of Caspar Milquetoast, the cartoon character? Scared little fella, always shakin' and whinin'. Nothin' like you," Rudy added quickly. He had a feeling if he ever wanted to see Hildy Helen again, he'd better be nice to this kid.

"Well, ya did good back there," Little Al said when they finally slowed down on a quiet side street. "If ya can't fight 'em with fists, ya might as well fight 'em with words. You had them goin'." Little Al stopped him under a streetlight and pointed. "That's Prairie Avenue. You live around here?"

Rudy looked up in surprise at his aunt's mansion, right on the corner opposite them.

"Right there," he said.

Little Al grunted. "Now what?"

"What do you mean?"

"You ain't gonna just waltz in the front door, are ya? I didn't drag you all this way so's you could go in and get caught anyway."

"What am I supposed to do, climb in through a window?"

"Sure," Little Al said. "I see one that'd be perfect."

Rudy remembered the street-level windows in the music room even before Little Al pointed. "I don't know if we can get in."

"Huh," Little Al said. "I can get in anywhere."

And it seemed he was right. Rudy couldn't even see his hand in front of him as they crept up to the music room window, but Little Al did some fiddling and had the window yawning open before Rudy could even glance over his shoulder twice.

"You'll fit through there," Little Al said. "Then you're on your own."

Rudy wriggled himself into position and turned to grin up at Little Al. "Thanks," he said.

But Little Al was already gone.

Rudy dropped down into the music room and scrambled up to close the window behind him. He held his breath as he waited for the footsteps that were sure to come across the hallway to the door. If Quintonia could hear what he was *thinking*, then surely she had just heard him fall to the rug with a thud.

But there wasn't a sound, nor did he hear anything as he crept up into the big hall and tiptoed toward the stairs. He almost made it to the bottom step when there was a sudden "Awk!"

"No, Picasso! Shhh!" Rudy whispered to him.

"Picasso, shhh!" the bird squawked out.

Rudy didn't wait for him to say more but sprang up the steps two at a time.

This is stupid, he thought as he slid into his room and shut the door soundlessly behind him. *They'll all be here in two seconds.*

But even after he'd wriggled out of his clothes and into his pajamas and gotten himself between the sheets and squeezed his eyes shut, no one threw open the door or turned on the light or said in a dry, crackly voice, "Rudolph, where have you *been*?"

The house was quiet as a cemetery.

And for the hours that crawled by before he drifted off into miserable sleep, Rudy thought he *was* going to die. It was obvious nobody cared where he was—thanks to Aunt Gussie. And if his flagpole-sitting caper didn't get her, nothing would. He was going to be stuck here—lost—forever. There was no point in even trying an emergency prayer.

He was awakened the next morning by the glare of sunlight suddenly flashing out from the shade that Quintonia had just sent rolling up into its holder.

"What?" Rudy said, pulling the pillow over his head.

"Ain't no 'what' about it," Quintonia said. "You best be gettin' your sweet self out of that bed, boy, 'cause you got to meet the delivery truck."

Rudy started to ask *what* delivery truck, but Quintonia marched out of the room before he could get the pillow off his head. He bolted up and ran to the window in time to see the truck in question. The words MONTGOMERY WARD were painted on the side, and it was pulling up to the front of the house.

"Come on!" Quintonia wailed from the stairs.

Still in his short-legged pajamas, Rudy hauled down after her. Hildy Helen was already at the front door, one hand clapped over her mouth, the other pointing outside.

"Rudy, look!" she said. "You don't think those are for us, do you?"

Rudy's eyes followed her pointing finger to a man in a green uniform who was walking up the drive carrying a shiny bicycle under each arm, one red, one blue. They were way too small for Dad, and Rudy frankly couldn't imagine Aunt Gussie on a two-wheeler. But the sting of yesterday was still sharp, and Rudy shook his head.

"I don't think so," he said. "I'll be lucky if she doesn't put me in the cage with Picasso."

"Don't think I didn't consider it," said the crackly voice behind him.

Aunt Gussie stepped briskly out into the sunlight and examined the two bicycles the uniformed man set down on the walk. Then with a "hmmph," she held out her hand, the man put a pad of paper into it, and she scratched across it with a pencil. As the man hurried back to his truck, Aunt Gussie turned to Rudy. Her sharp eyes bore through him like a pair of drills.

"Well, Rudolph," she said, "have you gotten it all out of your system now?"

Rudy nodded woodenly.

"Good, then," she said. She dusted her hands together. "Now, my second question: Can you ride a bicycle?"

Rudy nodded again.

"I know you can, Hildegarde, since you tried to make off with mine yesterday."

Rudy stared at his sister as she, too, nodded silently.

"I'm glad to know you can ride," Aunt Gussie said, giving the hands one more solid dusting, "because the way you two like to wander, I think you're both going to need these bicycles."

✢ ✢ ✢

Chapter Nine

$\mathcal{N}$ ow then," Aunt Gussie said, "my first rule about riding bicycles is that no one does it in pajamas or without breakfast. Get dressed and meet me in the dining room. We have a day to plan."

"I can't wait to see what her 'plan' is," Hildy Helen muttered to Rudy as they hurried up the stairs. "Something boring, no doubt."

"How come you didn't throw a tantrum yesterday to make her come after me?"

"I tried! She didn't even blink! I even started off after you myself on the bicycle I found in the garage, but I think she has eyes in the back of her head!"

"I could have been killed over there!"

"Don't I know it? But I heard her tell Dad she had everything under control—"

"She's a liar!" Rudy said. "And you know what? As soon as we're out there, I think we should ride straight to Indiana."

But Aunt Gussie had other plans, and she laid them out with the eggs and ham and bowls of berries, which Rudy ate like a starving man.

"You will find that weekends here are much different from the

73

weeks' activities," Aunt Gussie said. "We work hard all week, and we must play on Saturday and rest on Sunday. Now then, I think we shall start with the Municipal Pier. Eat your breakfast, Hildegarde. You're going to need your strength."

Strength wasn't what Rudy needed after breakfast was over and they stood out front with their new bicycles. What he needed was a sling to hold his mouth closed when Sol appeared around the side of the house with an elegant black bicycle, which Aunt Gussie promptly mounted and took off down the driveway on.

"Come along, children!" she called out. "And see that you keep up."

Rudy was hard put to do that as she sped to Michigan Avenue and then cut over to Lake Shore Drive. Before them stretched a wide, green, grassy band that Aunt Gussie announced was Grant Park, and beyond it, a sparkling, never ending sea of blue that she identified as Lake Michigan.

Rudy stole glances at the glittering lake while trying to navigate the in-and-out-of-traffic trail their aunt was leading them down. Sailboats were bobbing on the water, and bathers were chasing one another down the sand banks. Aunt Gussie got them quickly to the pier and stopped to let them have a look. The pier stretched out into the lake for what seemed like miles and boasted two story buildings with one especially big, dome-topped structure at the end.

"What's in it?" Hildy Helen said.

"Theaters," Aunt Gussie said. "A radio station. WCFL, the Voice of Labor."

Rudy's mind began to wander.

"Steamers, excursion boats. Have you children ever been on a boat?"

The twins shook their heads.

"Then there's that to be done. Come along, we'll park the bicycles here and take the streetcar down the pier."

Rudy was reluctant to let his new red bike out of his sight, but he let go of it pretty easily when he saw the streetcars, their tracks elevated above the pier as they raced at what looked like breakneck speed.

"Now, then, I want you to eat this on the way—you've burned up a good deal of energy," Aunt Gussie said and placed a Baby Ruth candy bar into each of their hands. Rudy stared at his.

"If you don't want it, Rudolph . . ." Aunt Gussie said.

But Rudy tore into the paper and shook his head.

"That's what I thought," she said. "Now I might as well tell you that I keep them in the bottom left-hand drawer of my desk in the library. You're certain to find them anyway." She squinted her eyes at the twins. "But keep your hands off. I know how many are in there at any given time."

The streetcar rocked its way down the track with Rudy holding on and Hildy Helen howling. Although he expected Aunt Gussie to tell her to hush up and mind her manners, the old lady only looked serenely out the window and then shooed them off the stopped car and down to a smaller pier, where she waved her gloves at a man in a blue coat and white cap. He grinned a semi-toothless smile and pointed up the gangplank.

"All aboard," Aunt Gussie said. "Time's wasting."

But time, as far as Rudy was concerned, stood still as they toured Lake Michigan on the trim white boat. He held on to a post and leaned out as far as he could, taking it all in.

The blue-green, choppy water, with seagulls sitting on it in stark white contrast and sailboats dipping on its surface was mesmerizing. So were the sounds of boat horns echoing across the water. Rudy wanted to sail to the breakwater beyond the pier, where Aunt Gussie said a person could fish.

She told them a number of things, actually, as they viewed the city from its banks. They learned there was no saltwater in Lake Michigan and no tide, and that the pier was soon going to have a new name, Navy Pier, to honor the sailors killed in the war.

But Rudy was much more interested in the way the city looked from here. The scariness was gone and in its place was a skyline that cut into the heavens like a big bread knife. He wished he'd brought his sketchbook so he could draw it.

"Look, there's a bunch of people swimming there!" Hildy Helen cried.

"That would be Oak Street Beach."

"It looks very modern," Hildy Helen said wistfully.

"It's the most fashionable beach in Chicago, if that's what you mean." Aunt Gussie gave a grunt and peered through the sunlight at the thin strip of sand where a throng of people in short-legged bathing suits splashed at the water's edge. "I have to say, those bathing outfits look practical for swimming, though. I never could abide those bathing skirts. A person can't swim worth a hoot in those." She gave one more grunt. "We'll have to put Oak Street Beach on our list then. But I want you to have a picture of the whole city in your minds, children. It's 189 square miles. A person could get hopelessly lost in it."

She cut her eyes slyly at Rudy and then pointed out across the water. "Now, you can see Grant Park from this angle. Notice the fountains and statues—"

"Notice the tennis courts!" Hildy Helen cried. "Oh, that looks like fun!"

"If you want to take a try at tennis, by all means I shall have to arrange lessons," Aunt Gussie said.

"Can you arrange for me to have my hair bobbed, too?" Hildy asked.

Aunt Gussie just grunted.

Hildy Helen went back to gazing at the tennis courts. Rudy looked at her closely.

She isn't starting to get along with Aunt Gussie, is she? he thought. No, it couldn't be. He and Hildy Helen always thought the same about the important things. *Nah, she's just trying to get on Aunt Gussie's good side so she can surprise her with something really wicked*, he decided. Hildy Helen was smart that way.

The cruise was over all too soon, and Rudy dragged his feet a little until they got into the bustle of the pier itself. A person, as Aunt Gussie put it, couldn't help but forget everything else in the midst of the crowds of smiling people, the tables for sitting and drinking lemonade and eating ice cream—both of which they did—and the puppet shows taking place outside the theaters. But it was the grand ballroom at the end that caught Hildy Helen.

The ballroom was a rounded sort of building, impressive in its big-windowed hugeness. Hildy Helen plastered her face against the glass, peered in, and let out a howl.

"They're dancing in there!" she cried.

"That is what one does in a ballroom, yes," Aunt Gussie said. "This one can hold 1,400 dancers."

"Is that the Charleston they're doing?" Hildy said.

Rudy watched the couples throwing their arms in the air and kicking up their feet to the strains of some fast, lively music.

"It is," Aunt Gussie said. Her eyes narrowed disapprovingly. "Silliest thing I ever saw."

"It's modern," Hildy Helen said.

"That doesn't necessarily make it art," Aunt Gussie said. "Now, ballet on the other hand—"

"I've never seen a ballet," Hildy Helen said.

"Say it isn't so!" Aunt Gussie cried. She was actually clutching the front of her blouse, her eyes bugging out in little points.

"It's so," Rudy said. "Thank heaven. It's just a bunch of people running around in their underwear."

"*Swan Lake* is on," Aunt Gussie said. "We shall see it tonight. If that catches your fancy as much as this ridiculous cavorting about," she said, jerking her gray head toward the ballroom, "then we shall see about dancing lessons for you as well."

Hildy Helen's eyes bulged. "Really?" she said.

Rudy's stomach churned. There was no mistaking it this time. Hildy Helen was being pulled like a fish on a pole out there on the breakwater.

"Of course, we'll have to discontinue the piano lessons," Aunt Gussie went on.

"That's fine with me!" Hildy Helen said.

Rudy flashed a quick, charming grin. "And it's fine with me if you stop the violin lessons, too."

Aunt Gussie looked at him thoughtfully. "Not just yet, Rudolph," she said after a minute. "I think we'll keep on with those."

Rudy opened his mouth to protest, but Aunt Gussie took them both firmly by the arm and said, "Now, have you ever had an Epsicle?"

Hildy Helen wrinkled her nose. "What's that?"

Aunt Gussie went on to describe a frozen concoction on a stick while Rudy fumed. *I suppose I could pretend to be all excited about tennis courts and ballets*, he thought. *But what good would that do? I'd just be trading the violin for a pair of stockings!*

In spite of how good the Epsicle did turn out to be, so cool and sweet in his mouth, the rest of the day was clouded for Rudy. He pouted all through Lincoln Park, where the smells of German food and the sounds of jazz both roared from every doorway; all the while they were wheeling their bicycles through the fancy, modern North Side; and every moment of their ride along the green Chicago River with its tall, streamlined buildings and ornate bridges. Through it all, Hildy Helen seemed to grow more at ease pedaling alongside Aunt Gussie.

Not Rudy. The minute they got back to Prairie Avenue, he escaped to his room and drew until supper time. He sketched Aunt

Gussie and Sol and Quintonia and Leo all chasing each other crazily across a city full of buildings with tongues waggling out their windows. It didn't make him feel any better.

He felt even worse after that evening's excursion to the ballet. Hildy Helen oohed and aahed over the Chicago Cultural Center and stared up at its stained-glass dome until Rudy was sure she'd have a crick in her neck. When the ballet started, she sat with her eyes glued to the figures who, just as he suspected, twirled around on the stage in what looked like underwear to him. All the way home she gushed about how beautiful it all was, and she wandered off to her room, starry-eyed, without even asking Rudy what he'd thought.

Rudy scribbled a cartoon featuring Aunt Gussie in a tutu and went to bed feeling strangely lonely.

The next morning, if possible, was worse. After breakfast, Aunt Gussie inspected both of them and made them change their clothes twice until they met her approval—and to Rudy's relief, even Hildy Helen was groaning. Then she carted them off to church in the Pierce Arrow, with Dad in tow as well. As always, Aunt Gussie grilled the children.

"You've been to church before, I presume," she said.

"Church?" Rudy said. Of course he had. Their father had seen to it that they attended service every Sunday—and Sunday school, too. But he had to find some fun somewhere or he was going to explode. "Church?" he said again. "You mean, where you sing hymns and pray and listen to a sermon?"

"Yes."

"Nope," he said. "Never been."

Aunt Gussie looked at Hildy, who in turn, looked as if she were being torn in half. Rudy was disappointed that she even hesitated before saying, "We're practically orphans, you know."

"I'm certain you don't know how to behave in church then," Aunt Gussie said, and she went on to list 20 or 30 "thou shalt nots," all of which Rudy ignored.

It wasn't that he didn't respect God. He believed in Him, that was for sure. Why else would he pray all those emergency prayers? He knew just about every Bible story backward and forward, and a few Bible verses, too. His attitude was that God must come in pretty handy, since Rudy was still alive and had yet to be thrown in jail.

But church was boring, and Rudy sat in the pew, swinging his legs and dreaming about what they would do if he and Hildy Helen could somehow get into those beams way up in the ceiling. What could a person drop on an unsuspecting congregation?

He wished he'd paid more attention, however, when they sat down at the dinner table and Aunt Gussie began the grilling.

"What was the topic of today's sermon?" she said while Dad was slicing the roast.

"The price of salami," Rudy said, his face as serious as he could keep it. He wasn't sure exactly what salami was, but he knew it was some kind of food.

He sneaked a glance at Hildy Helen. She chewed for a moment and then said, "No—it was the dance of Salome. See, Herod liked her dancing so much, he promised to give her anything she wanted."

"Excellent, Hildegarde," Aunt Gussie said. "Now then—"

Rudy stared at his sister. She looked at him across the table, her brown eyes innocent. Although Rudy furrowed his brow at her, she just blinked and turned to Aunt Gussie.

"I have a question, Auntie," she said.

Auntie? She's Auntie *now?* Rudy wanted to shout at her.

"You may ask me anything," Aunt Gussie said.

"Why are the women in the Bible so evil? Why don't they ever talk about any good women?"

"Superb question!" Aunt Gussie said. Rudy actually thought he saw the hint of a smile playing at her lips.

"May I be excused?" Rudy said suddenly.

"Before dessert?" Dad said. "Feel his forehead, Quintonia. See if the boy's ill."

"I'm not ill. I just—can I go ride my bike?"

"May I?" Aunt Gussie said.

"Yeah," Rudy said.

Aunt Gussie watched him for a minute, and then she nodded. "But don't go anywhere we haven't been. I haven't finished showing you the city yet."

Rudy headed for the door, hoping that Hildy Helen would excuse herself, too, and follow him. But when he glanced back, she was leaning on her elbows, her eyes riveted to Aunt Gussie, her next question already halfway out. Rudy's stomach shivered, and he left for the West Side, in search of Little Al.

Chapter Ten

*I*t took a while for Rudy to find his way back to Hull House and then to the street where Little Al had hailed his uncle in his taxicab. When he hit Taylor Street with its row of Sunday-quiet groceries and bakeries, the first thing he saw were two of Little Al's friends.

They were slouched against the front of a closed newsstand, sharing a cigarette, their eyes restlessly scanning the street. When they saw him, they were up on their feet.

You can't let them think you're a sissy, Little Al had said.

Rudy shoved his curls under his cap and, dismounting the bike, swaggered toward them. He hoped he looked like Little Al.

The taller one smirked. "Hey, 'Rudolph,' " he said. "Where's yer big, fancy car today?"

Rudy's heart dropped to his gut. "I let the old lady use it," he said. "Otherwise, I'd take you two fellas for a spin."

The shorter boy actually looked disappointed. The other one jabbed him in the ribs with his elbow. "Yeah, but we'll let you make it up to us," he said. "No hard feelings."

"Well, aren't you just the cat's pajamas?" Rudy said. "No, make that the bee's knees. The elephant's eyebrow—"

"Dummy up, would ya?"

"The butterfly's boots?"

"Shut up!"

Rudy did, and began to back the bike away.

"Knock him over, Vincie," the tall boy said. "Bet he's got some clams on him."

"No clams," Rudy said, his heart pounding but mouth grinning. "Now, oysters—"

Vincie flopped a hand over his mouth and began fumbling in Rudy's pockets. When he came up empty-handed, he gave Rudy a shove, right into the other kid, who looked down at him with small, mean eyes. Rudy heard his bicycle crash to the sidewalk.

"How come you're goin' around with no cash, rich boy?" he said.

"Yeah," Vincie said, standing on his tiptoes for effect, "we've bumped off people for less than that, ain't we, Danny?"

Rudy's mind raced. "Hasn't Little Al told you?" he said. "He's keepin' an eye on my money from now on. Matter of fact, I was hopin' you fellas could tell me where I could find him right now."

"Over at his Uncle Anthony's store," Vincie said.

Danny gave him a sharp jab.

Rudy broke into a grin. "Thanks, I gotta be goin'," he said.

"Where do you think you're goin'?" Danny said.

But Rudy was already going there. He snatched up his bike and started riding while he was still getting on, darting it in front of a car and disappearing into the alley while Danny and Vincie waited for the angry driver to move on.

This oughta be about the back of Uncle Anthony's store, Rudy thought as he leaned the bike against a building. Now he had to find a way to get Little Al's attention.

He picked up a handful of gravel and was about to hurl it at a dusty window when the back screen door came open and Little Al himself appeared.

"My uncle gets in a lather when people throw rocks at his

windows," he said, his mouth barely moving. "You want some salami?"

He sat down on the back step in the alley with a knife and a hunk of meat and pared off a slice, which he held out to Rudy. Rudy took it and let his teeth sink into it. He had, after all, skipped dessert, and this was some of the best stuff he'd ever put into his mouth. So *this* was salami.

Little Al chewed contentedly. "How'd you find me?"

"Danny and Vincie told me. I had to trick them into it."

Little Al's eyes sparked up from the salami. "How'd you do that?"

Rudy told him, and Little Al gave him his tight little smile. "Huh," he said.

"So," Rudy said, "how come you don't hang out at your own house?"

Little Al concentrated on the paring knife. "My father, he died couple years ago. I don't get along so good with my stepfather." He shrugged. "I don't go home that much. Hey, since you're so good at scams, you wanna learn the moll buzz?"

"I don't know. What's a moll buzz?"

Little Al disappeared inside the grocery and returned minus the salami and the knife, but carrying a shopping bag.

"You can leave the bike here," he said.

"You sure?"

"Can't use it in this game. Now, all we gotta do is find a lady with a baby carriage," Little Al said as they emerged from the alley onto Taylor Street. Rudy looked around nervously for Danny and Vincie, but the street was Sunday-afternoon empty.

"Plenty of 'em over Sheridan Park," Al said and led the way.

There were several women pushing carriages in the lazy heat, and Little Al picked out one and pointed to her with his chin.

"See that doll over there?" he said. "Go over there and ask her for directions to Bishop Street. And be real stupid about it. You don't get it the first three or four times she tries to explain it to ya, got it?"

"Sure, but why?" Rudy said.

Little Al grinned. "You'll see. But make sure she stays facin' this way."

"Got it," Rudy said. From the gleam in Little Al's eyes, whatever this trick was, it was going to be split-your-sides funny. He couldn't help wishing Hildy Helen were here to howl over it with him.

Yeah—but when I get home and tell her about it, he thought, *she'll forget the stupid ballet lessons and tennis lessons and want to be back with me.*

"Go," Little Al said.

Rudy strode toward the lady in the red-checked dress and squinted around.

"Excuse me, miss?" he said.

She looked up absently from the carriage, and Rudy flashed a charmer smile. Her eyes narrowed suspiciously, but she gave a cautious nod.

"I hate to bother you, but I'm trying to find Bishop Street. Could you tell me—"

"Sure, but I don't know how you missed it coming from that direction. You'd have to be blind."

She went on clipping out her words, and Rudy went on nodding stupidly. Just like Little Al said, he made her tell him three times, and by then she was sighing impatiently.

"What are ya, deaf?" she said. "I told you—"

"Thanks, thanks a lot," Rudy said. He gave her one more smile and looked around for Little Al. When, he wondered, were they going to get to the funny part?

But Little Al was nowhere in sight, and the lady in the red and white dress was already moving the carriage on down the walkway.

Rudy headed off in the direction she'd sent him in. When he got to the edge of the park, a hand reached out from behind a park bench and grabbed him. Rudy stifled a yell as he realized it was Little Al.

"Nice work," Al said. "We make good partners, you and me."

"What are you talking about?" Rudy said. "I didn't see anything funny about that, except it made a fool outta *me!*"

"I wasn't lookin' for laughs," Little Al said through his teeth. "I was lookin' for this."

Rudy looked down and blinked at what Little Al held in his hands. "That's somebody's pocketbook," he said.

"Yeah, the dame with the baby. They always carry them in the carriage, see? While you were askin' for directions, I nabbed it and stuck it in the shopping bag. You didn't even notice me, did ya?"

"No."

"Neither did she. You had her hook, line, and sinker."

Little Al stuck out his hand, and Rudy looked at it blankly.

"Shake," Little Al said. "We're partners."

Rudy felt his stomach doing a somersault. "Partners—in stealing?" he said.

"If you wanna call it that," Little Al said, digging through the bag. "Hey, look at this! Five clams! I'll hafta get change so we can split it."

Rudy shook his head.

"No, you keep it all," he said.

"How come?"

"Because that was stealing. I never did that before."

Little Al shrugged and stuck the bill into his pocket. "Suit yourself," he said. "C'mon, let's go to the sittin' wall and look at the rest of this stuff."

Rudy must have cast a dozen uneasy glances over his shoulders as he followed Little Al to a wall that rose above the railroad tracks. He settled himself beside the little Italian and watched as he dug through the handbag with expert hands.

"Nah, nothin' much," Al said finally, " 'cept this almond bar. Y'want some?"

Rudy had a ball of fear the size of Shelbyville in his stomach. He shook his head. Little Al unwrapped the candy and went to work on it.

"So, I guess this was your first caper, huh?" he said.

"If you mean robbery, yeah," Rudy said. He worked his shoulders nervously.

"Well, that was nothin'," Little Al said. "Small-time stuff. What I want to do is big touches, like the Boss does. Let me tell you about Capone." His voice took on an awed tone, and Rudy watched as his eyes grew dreamy with admiration. "See, Al, he's the biggest gangster ever was. He owns Chicago!"

"Says you!"

"He's got millions of dollars, can make anybody do what he wants. There's seven hundred gunmen in his army. And I'm gonna be one of them, soon as I'm tall enough."

"Why would you want to do that?" Rudy said.

"Because I ain't gonna end up poor like my mother and get pushed around like my old man did. I want power, see? And that's what Al Capone's got. If you work for him, you got power, too, see?"

Rudy shrugged. He was glad a train chose that moment to clatter by so he didn't have to answer. By the time it had passed, Little Al was back to his description.

"He always wears silk shirts and a diamond-studded belt," Little Al said. "Some people say he wears silk underwear, but he doesn't spend all his money on himself."

"No?"

"I heard that on Christmas Eve, he'll give a cab driver a

hundred dollar tip because he has to be out there workin' instead
of home with his family."

"Oh," Rudy said. "But doesn't he mostly do illegal stuff—even
kill people?"

Little Al brushed that aside with his hand as if it were an un-
important detail. "But what I like about him is he's unique, see—
one of a kind. He ain't afraid to take risks." He looked up at Rudy
through squinted eyes. "That's what I like about you, too."

"Me?"

"Yeah. You took a chance comin' down here. You ain't gonna
let your old lady turn you into a sissy. You got what it takes,
Rudolpho."

"You're right about one thing," Rudy said. "She is trying to
turn me into a sissy. She even made me go to the ballet last
night."

Little Al snorted. "I wouldn'ta let her. Now the opera would
be different."

"You'd go to the opera?"

"You bet! All the mobsters love the opera, see? Al Capone's
got his own seat."

Rudy casually inspected the toes of his shoes. "So, you think
I'm like him—Al Capone?"

"Sure, y'are. And that's why you and me, we make good partners."

That was why, as Rudy retrieved his bike from behind the grocery store and rode back to Prairie Avenue, he didn't think about
Little Al and him stealing a purse from the lady in the red and
white checked dress. He thought about taking risks.

"Aunt Gussie," he said when he found her reading in the library with Picasso on her shoulder, "do you like the opera?"

"Who wants to know?" she said.

"Well, me."

Her sharp eyes darted over the tops of her glasses. "You want to go to the opera, Rudolph?" she said.

"Opera, Rudolph?" Picasso squawked. "Opera?"

"Yeah," Rudy said.

Aunt Gussie removed her glasses and stood up briskly. "Then we shall go tonight," she said. "We'll have to take a cab. Your father is off having supper with—"

"Where's Sol?"

"The servants have a day of rest, too. Which means we shall have to eat out. The Cape Cod Room, I believe. Have you ever tasted Italian food, Rudolph?"

"I've had salami."

"Just recently, too, from the smell of you. This will be different. Put your church clothes back on. And wash. You look like a dead-end kid."

Aunt Gussie wasn't kidding about the Cape Cod Room being different from sitting on the back stoop of Little Al's uncle's grocery store sharing a hunk of salami. Attached to the Drake Hotel, it was a place of quiet elegance with white linen tablecloths and a man playing the violin among the tables. Rudy wasn't surprised to see that it was Leo.

The place was dimly lit and glowing with candles. There was none of the roughness of Little Italy—no hoodlums lurking in the shadows, no loud shouting across the room, no strong odor of salami. The pasta and garlic-filled red sauce ringed in golden olive oil was served on china plates by thin men in tuxedos, and all the customers were dressed in silk and sported pearls.

One group in particular caught Rudy's ear. It was a quartet of men sitting at a table against the back wall, some of them talking in voices that sounded vaguely familiar to Rudy. Where had he heard that stones-in-a-bucket tone before?

Rudy watched them as, dressed in white fedoras and wearing red carnations in their lapels, they had tray after tray of steaming crabs and fettucine served to them. Every time they moved their hands, their fingers caught the light with their diamonds and rubies.

"Rudolph, it is not polite to stare," Aunt Gussie said.

Hildy Helen turned to see, too. Rudy was glad she was showing some interest.

"What were you looking at?" she whispered to him when Aunt Gussie's attention was distracted by Leo.

Just as she asked, one of the men, the quietest one, raised his arm to summon the waiter, and Rudy caught a glimpse of his belt buckle, shimmering in the candlelight. It was diamond-studded.

"He's an oily-looking fellow," Hildy Helen whispered, nose wrinkled.

"That's not just some fellow," Rudy said. "That's Al Capone."

"So?" Hildy Helen said. "Who's he?"

Rudy tried to puff out his chest, the way Little Al did. "He's a man who dares to take risks and be unique," he said. "You know, kind of like me."

"Rudolph, what's the matter?" Aunt Gussie said, pointing to his expanded chest. "Are you having trouble breathing in all this cigar smoke?"

After the lasagna and the spumoni ice cream, Aunt Gussie and the twins climbed into a closed cab—not at all like Uncle Gino's shabby one—and went to the Civic Opera House. It was another dripping-with-wealth kind of place, but that didn't get the excitement running up Rudy's backbone, nor did the opera itself. It was some story about a servant guy who ran around making people fall in love, which, frankly, made Rudy want to draw cartoons of Figaro being put to his death.

He really didn't see what Little Al would find so swell about all this, but as he cast around in boredom for something to think about, his eyes hung up on a balcony that bowed out over the rest of the audience to their right. Sitting there in high-backed chairs that looked a whole lot more comfortable than the seat Rudy was squirming in, were the four men he'd seen in the restaurant. Even from where he sat, Rudy could see tears gleaming on their oily cheeks. The man with the diamond belt buckle wiped his face with a silk handkerchief that matched his necktie.

"Rudolph, what are you staring at *now?*" Aunt Gussie said.

Rudy blinked in the glare of the sudden lights that came on. "Is one of those men Al Capone? Are those mobsters?"

Aunt Gussie took him by the shoulder with a hand that felt like an iron wrench and steered him up the aisle. "Rudolph," she said, mouth pulled in prune fashion, "do not waste your good mind on things like that. Now, then, how did you like the opera?"

"I don't want to waste my good mind on things like *that*, either," Rudy said.

He waited for Aunt Gussie to launch into a lecture so he could mimic her behind her back and get Hildy Helen to giggling. But his aunt merely said, "Hmm," and hailed a cab.

"Dad's home!" Hildy Helen said when they opened the front door on Prairie Avenue.

Rudy heard his voice, too, talking excitedly in the library. They both nearly knocked down Aunt Gussie getting to him. It felt as if days had gone by since they'd seen him.

Dad glanced up from the leather chair, where he was deep in conversation with a stranger and, for a moment, looked at the twins as if they were people he had never seen before. He did that when he was deep in his work, which was usually.

The man he was talking to took a greater interest in them. He stood up, beaming out a smile from a wreath of wrinkles, and held out a beefy hand to Rudy. His handshake was enough to crush a couple of fingers.

"Are you a boxer?" Rudy said.

The man let out a wonderful wheezy laugh, and blue eyes twinkled down at Rudy. "That's the nicest thing anybody has said to me all day! I *was* a boxer in my day, which was quite a few days ago, believe me!"

"Then who are you?" Hildy Helen said, squeezing in beside Rudy.

"You'll have to excuse my children's manners," Dad said.

Rudy scowled. Until they'd come here to Aunt Gussie's, their father had never cared a fig about manners.

"Not at all!" the ex-boxer said. "I like outspokenness, especially in a woman."

"That's why he likes me," Aunt Gussie said as she sailed into the room. "Good evening, Judge Caduff! I was hoping James would bring you by, although I'm sure he hasn't offered you a single thing to eat or drink."

"Judge Caduff worked in your grandfather's law firm here in Chicago when he was just a boy," Dad said to the twins.

"Austin Hutchinson was a fine man—fine man," the judge said. "Learned everything I know that's of any importance from him. Law school was a perfect waste of time."

"Your father wouldn't want to hear you say that," Aunt Gussie said. "You know how he felt about education."

Rudy shuffled his feet. He'd much rather hear about Judge Caduff's boxing days than about some dusty old relative's views on school.

"As a matter of fact, James and I were just talking about that," Judge Caduff said, waving Aunt Gussie into a chair. "I also know what Austin Hutchinson would have said about boys no older than this one here," he jabbed a thumb toward Rudy, "being thrown in prison with hardened criminals and coming out like little Al Capones."

"Al Capone! Rat-tat-tat!" Picasso cried. He sounded for all the world like the gun Rudy had heard go off at Union Station. It suddenly occurred to him where he'd heard that stones-in-a-bucket voice before.

"Some boys might not think that was so bad," Rudy said.

Dad looked at him, and Judge Caduff's blue eyes clouded over. "No?" he said.

Rudy shook his head. "I have a friend, just my age, who *wants* to be like Al Capone. I bet he'd volunteer to go to prison if he thought he'd come out that tough."

"Rudy!" Dad said.

Rudy certainly had his full attention now. But the judge put up his hand and beckoned for Rudy to come closer.

"You, too, honey," he said to Hildy Helen. His face was somber as they stood facing him. "If you knew what it was truly like to be a member of the mob, you wouldn't say that, son. You'd do everything you could to keep your friend away from those people and their terrible business."

"And that's what *we're* about," Dad said. "The only way to stop the mob is to keep it from getting any new life—"

"And destroying *more* lives."

That's not the way Little Al told it, Rudy thought later as he sketched some drawings of the men crying at the opera and Judge Caduff standing in the boxing ring wearing gloves and a judge's robe. *Who's right?*

There was only one way to know, he decided. And that was to find out for himself.

✜ ✜ ✜

Chapter Eleven

*T*he next day at Hull House, as soon as Aunt Gussie had turned them loose and Hildy Helen got interested in the Doll Club meeting, Rudy went to look for Little Al.

It took most of the morning, but a trail of questions finally led him to the clubhouse Little Al had built with the other Italian boys. Rudy spotted Danny and Vincie and ducked behind a big piece of tin roofing that was being used as a wall. When somebody tapped his shoulder, he jumped a foot. But it was Little Al.

"Whatta ya doin'?" Al said. "Spyin' on me?"

"Just looking for you. I've been thinking about us being partners."

"Yeah?"

Rudy looked around for Danny and Vincie, but they were busy pretending to beat up some kid, who was obliging them by pretending to be in great pain.

"We need to talk private," Little Al said. "Come on, we'll go to my office."

His "office" turned out to be the landing on the fire escape near where Rudy had spent the day on the flagpole. He tried not to think about that.

"So," Al said when they were settled with the usual hunk of

salami and knife pulled from Little Al's pocket. "You gonna do it?"

"I don't know. I saw Al Capone—well, I think I saw him, at the opera last night, and he did look pretty swell."

Little Al shook his head in awe. "Didn't that make you want to join right up when you saw that diamond-studded belt buckle?"

"That was swell, all right. But then I got home, and— "

He told Little Al about what the judge had said. He wasn't some codger with a hook nose, Rudy assured him. He was a pretty all right guy himself.

But Little Al scowled down at the last hunk of salami before he crammed it into his mouth and licked the grease from his fingertips. "He don't know what he's talkin' about, that judge," he said with his mouth full. "He don't know nothin' about the thrill of the underworld—or else he does and he just hates us Italians, just like most of them do."

"I don't think that's it," Rudy said.

"Yeah, it is. See, them types, they want to see us be good little wops and shine shoes and sell papers and clean streets. Huh!" Al eliminated those possibilities with a wave of his cleanly-licked fingers. "If we work for the mob, see, then we know too much. We're as smart and powerful and rich as them. That's why I've already started."

"Started what?"

"Provin' myself."

"To Al Capone?"

"Not to the Boss himself, 'course not. But to some of the fellas that work for him, helpin' run scams and such."

Little Al removed his hat to check his hair. Rudy suddenly had a picture of Al in his mind, wearing a fedora and crying at the opera.

"Havin' anything you want," Al said. "Bein' able to do whatever you want, whenever you want. Havin' people do what *you* say for a change. Wouldn't that give you a thrill, Rudolpho? Especially after seein' them fellas last night?"

Rudy had to admit it might. But he studied the dusty toe of his high-tops.

"You think too much about things bein' against the law," Little Al said.

"My father's a lawyer," Rudy said. "That's all I hear about!"

Little Al leaned back against the brick wall of Hull House and crossed his feet up on the fire escape rail. His hands went lazily behind his head. All he needed was a cigar hanging from his mouth to complete the picture.

"We could get around that," he said.

"How?" Rudy said.

"Well, you wouldn't have to actually *do* the stealin' or nothin'. You could do what you done the other day, when we pulled off the moll buzz. You could always be the stall. I never done it so easy as I done it with you. You got the character for it, see? I bet you could set me up for a grift so nice. And even if I was to get caught—which I wouldn't, of course—*you* wouldn't because you wouldn't be the one doin' the liftin'.'"

"Grift?" Rudy said.

"Small stuff. Pickin' pockets, like that. We could probably pull off two or three this afternoon! Just think of it as one of your pranks you pull on people. Only you get more than just a laugh out of it, see?"

Little Al's eyes had taken on a gleam that was pulling at Rudy like a rubber band going in two directions. Helping to pick someone's pocket—that was as scary a thing as Rudy could think of. And yet it did send a thrill up his backbone like nothing he'd ever felt. Both feelings were churning right in the middle of his stomach.

Little Al was watching him shrewdly. "So what do you say?"

"Can't do it today," Rudy said.

"How come?"

"I'm not saying. You'll laugh, and then I'll have to black your eye."

"Says you! Come on, I won't laugh. We're partners, remember?"

Rudy rolled his eyes in disgust. "I have to take my violin lesson."

"You get to take violin lessons?"

"Get to?" Rudy said. "I'd rather have my head shaved."

"Not me!" Little Al got up on his knees and opened his mouth farther than Rudy had ever seen it go. He ran an excited hand across his slicked-back hair. "I'd give up my left hook if I could learn to play the violin!" he said.

"Are you off your nut? Why would a tough guy like you want to waste your time taking lessons on a stupid—"

"Because the quality mobsters like Al Capone, see, they love a guy who can make a violin sing. They love it almost as much as the opera."

Rudy snorted. "Too bad you're not the one living at my Aunt Gussie's then."

"Shh!" Al said, putting his hand on Rudy's arm.

Rudy followed his gaze to the street below where a woman was hurrying down the sidewalk hauling a chubby little boy by the hand.

"What?" Rudy whispered.

"Perfect mark," Little Al said. "You see that handbag hangin' over her shoulder?"

"Yeah, I see it," Rudy said. "It's wide open!"

Little Al looked at him and smiled his tight little smile. "Rudolpho, I think you're the perfect gentleman to go down there and tell her that very thing."

Rudy's stomach did a one-and-a-half gainer. "I don't know."

"You go down and give her that big stupid grin you're always flashin' around and tell her you're real concerned because you saw something fall out of her bag about a half a block back, right in front of Geis's."

"The pastry shop?" Rudy said. "I don't see anything there."

"Of course you don't, knucklehead! But I'll be waitin' in the doorway when she gets there and starts searching, and while I'm plucking something out of her bag and droppin' it on the ground for her to find, I'll also be liftin' something for us. See?"

Rudy's insides were in knots, but Little Al seemed to know just how to untie them. "Tell you what," he said. "You try it this once. If yer conscience starts eatin' at ya, you're out of it—no hard feelings. If you find out you like it, you're already on your way. "

"To what?" Rudy said.

"To the big touch—the one that'll set us up for life so we never have to work again—legal or illegal." Little Al's eyes darted to the sidewalk below, where the hurried mother had stopped at the vegetable stand and was trying to pry an apple out of her child's hand. "You better decide fast 'cause that mark ain't gonna be there forever."

"It really is like playing a trick, right?"

"Sure. It's what she gets for bein' careless, see?"

Little Al gave him a knowing look, as if they shared a secret no one else knew. The knots in Rudy's stomach loosened, and he felt his face go into a grin. There wasn't a trace of a left-out feeling as he hurried down the fire escape steps and ran across the street toward the now very red-faced mother.

"Howie, no!" she was snarling at the little boy. "You had enough to eat! You'd think you had a hollow leg!"

"Madam?" Rudy said in a voice he knew even Aunt Gussie would approve of. "I couldn't help but notice—I think you dropped something back there."

She scowled down the sidewalk toward the pastry shop. "I don't see nothin'."

"I sure thought it was money," Rudy said. "I didn't dare pick it up. I thought maybe you'd think I was trying to steal it."

Her eyebrows shot up, and her eyes glowed with that kind of look Old Miss Cross-Eyes used to give him when he brought her an apple. He smothered a smile.

"Where did you say it was?" she said.

"Back there in front of Geis's Bakery," Rudy said. "Right near the gutter," he added quickly. Little Al would want her back to him, after all.

I am pretty good at this, aren't I? he thought smugly.

"Thank you, son," she said and abruptly whipped the little boy away from the fruit bin and rushed back toward the bakery. The noon whistle blew just as Rudy reached the other side of the street to watch from Little Al's "office." People would start pouring out of Hull House any minute, which could create good cover for Little Al.

Just in case, though, Rudy thought as he reached for the bottom of the fire escape, *I could warn him if it looks like anybody's about to catch him.* Next time, he decided, they were going to have to have some signals.

But signals and next times suddenly disappeared from Rudy's mind. For just as he reached the bottom step and turned to survey Little Al again, a tall, stiff figure stalked across the street, its sensible black pumps tapping like a judge's gavel.

"Excuse me, ma'am!" Aunt Gussie's voice crackled above the traffic. "Did you know your pocketbook is hanging wide open?"

The woman whirled around, startled, to look at her gaping handbag. Rudy nearly lost his hold on the railing as Little Al smoothly stepped back into the shadows of Geis's doorway and disappeared inside. Rudy could see him through the window, looking for all the world as if he were selecting just the right cream puff for his lunch.

"That must be how my money fell out!" Rudy heard the woman cry. "Do you see it anywhere? That nice young man told me it was here."

To Rudy's horror, instead of looking in the gutter for her money, she scanned the street and pointed right at him.

"That boy there!" she cried. "He told me he saw me drop it here. But someone must have picked it up already."

Aunt Gussie spent only a split second glaring at Rudy before she began to survey the street. Like a magnet, her eyes picked up the figure in the bakery.

"Oh, no," Rudy moaned.

"What's wrong?"

It was Hildy Helen, suddenly beside him. Rudy grabbed her arm. "Trouble," he said. "I gotta help."

"Rudy Hutchinson, what are you up to now?"

"Nothing," he snapped at her and took off across the street.

By the time he reached Geis's, the lady with the purse had already rushed away, dragging the little boy and muttering about money she hadn't even lost. Aunt Gussie had opened the bakery door and was barking dry-crisp orders inside.

"Alonzo Delgado, come out here immediately."

Rudy froze on the sidewalk, barely aware that Hildy Helen had breathlessly caught up to him. To his amazement, Little Al did emerge, nonchalantly licking the sugar off a cream puff Rudy was certain he hadn't paid for.

"You call me?" he said, his lips barely moving.

"You know I did, and I think you know why," Aunt Gussie said.

"Guess I'm stupid then," Little Al said, " 'cause I don't know nothin' about nothin'."

"You know nothing about that poor woman who thinks she lost her money on the sidewalk?"

"She did?" Little Al smirked, and he took to searching the ground with hungry eyes. Aunt Gussie was apparently not fooled, because she took up his chin in her palm and drilled her eyes into his. His smirk twisted into a scowl that made Rudy take a step backward, right onto Hildy Helen's foot.

"Ouch!" she whispered. "Who is that character, anyway?"

"That's the oldest trick in the book, Mr. Delgado," Aunt Gussie said. "Don't try it around here again. What I do suggest you try is putting forth more of an effort in your music class. Miss Martha Smith says you have stopped participating altogether."

"Yeah, yeah, yeah," Little Al said. "Now if there's nothin' else, lady, I gotta be goin'."

Aunt Gussie grunted, and Little Al sauntered off down the sidewalk. As she watched him go, Hildy Helen jabbed Rudy in her favorite rib-poking place. "Who *is* that, Rudy?" she said.

"Yes, Rudolph," Aunt Gussie said. She tilted her chin sharply from under her stern gray hat. "I presume you have made his acquaintance."

Rudy tried to smirk, Little Al fashion. "Maybe I have," he said.

"Then maybe you ought to forget completely that you ever saw him. I don't want you hanging about with the likes of him. There are plenty of other good boys here at Hull House who are trying to make decent lives for themselves. Choose some of *them* as playmates, but stay as far away from Alonzo Delgado as you can."

With that, she turned on her sensible heel and marched toward the car, where Sol was waiting with the door open. Rudy didn't move. Hildy Helen poked him again.

"Well," she said.

"Well, what?"

"Are you going to do it? Are you going to stay away from that boy?"

Rudy's stomach was churning so hard he was sure he was

going to throw up, right there in front of Geis's Bakery. But he tilted his chin up every bit as sharply as Aunt Gussie and looked at his sister.

"No," he said. "But I'm going to stay as far away from *her* as I can." With a grunt of his own, Rudy brushed past her and stomped toward the Pierce Arrow.

It was hard to stay out of Gussie Nitz's hawk-like sight. It was so hard, in fact, that by the next morning, Rudy knew he would explode if he had to sit in the Pierce Arrow with her. When breakfast was over and he had taken the shortest bath he could get away with, he took himself into the library where she was reading the morning mail and said, "I'm going to ride my bicycle to Hull House today."

She lifted both eyebrows above her spectacles. Her look made Picasso ruffle his feathers and scurry to the back of his cage, but Rudy was ready for her. He had a cricket in one pocket—he'd heard Quintonia say they loved to chew on old books—and a couple of marbles in the other—sure to put the scare into the old lady if he threatened to launch them at one of her stupid old urns. It was time to dig deeper into the Rudy Hutchinson bag of tricks.

Aunt Gussie straightened her glasses and went back to her letter. "Then I suppose you'd better be on your way. It could take some time what with the morning traffic. The way the automobiles have taken over, we'll be needing those red and green lights at every corner before you know it."

"So, I can?" Rudy said.

He wanted to bite his tongue off as Aunt Gussie lips twitched. "That's an interesting question, Rudolph," she said. "I don't recall your asking permission in the first place. Will Hildegarde be going with you?"

At that, Rudy's heart sank a little, and he shrugged. "I don't know," he said. "I didn't ask her."

For the first time, Aunt Gussie's eyes flickered surprise. It suddenly hurt too much to stand there any longer, so Rudy jammed his hat onto his curls and said, "I'll be seein' ya then."

Before she could add any more instructions, Rudy was out the door, headed for his bike.

He'd never ridden in the hustle of cars and buses full of people going to their jobs. The odor of gasoline mixed with the always-there stench of the stockyards and factories went up Rudy's nose the way spinach went down his throat gagging all the way. Between that and the horns that blasted at him every time he tried to ride across an intersection, he had to stuff down the question: *Is this really worth it?*

Of course it is, he told himself sternly. *Hildy's gone and hooked herself up with Aunt Gussie. Dad's so busy with his office, he's forgotten we're alive. Aunt Gussie's dead set on turning me into a violin-playing Milquetoast. I can't even pull off a prank!*

Except with Little Al. And that was who he was looking for as he leaned his bike against the wall under his friend's "office" and tucked his curls tight back under his cap.

But Little Al wasn't holding office hours yet—and when Rudy went reluctantly inside Hull House when he saw the Pierce Arrow coming down the street, he didn't find him in there, either. Evidently, Aunt Gussie's instructions had fallen on deaf ears, because he never did appear for the boys' singing class.

Danny and Vincie were there, however, and once they discovered Rudy at the edge of the room, they never took their marble-hard eyes off him. Rudy squirmed, but he held himself fast on the wooden folding chair. Once Little Al showed up, he'd have protection. Meanwhile, he started searching his head for the next step. If he was going to be partners with Little Al, he was going to have to be smarter than this.

When the lunch whistle blew, Rudy was the first one to bolt from the room. One glance over his shoulder, however, told him

Danny and Vincie were fighting the crowd to get to him. Their faces were pointed like weasels.

As soon as he got out into the hall, Rudy shut the door behind him, setting up a wail of protests from inside. While half a dozen boys scuffled to get it open, Rudy dove behind a tall wastepaper basket and waited.

By the time the door was finally wrenched open—with Miss Martha Smith half-singing, half-screeching instructions above their shouting—Danny and Vincie were at the front of the throng, and just as Rudy had hoped, they took off down the hall like a pair of bloodhounds. Rudy smirked to himself and hoped he looked at least a tiny bit like Little Al.

"Rudy, *what* are you doing?"

"Shh!" Rudy hissed, and he pulled his sister down behind the trash can with him.

She grinned. "What prank do you have going?" she said. "Let me in on it!"

Her eyes were twinkling, and for a minute there it was like it had always been with them. For a minute there, Rudy almost told her. Until she spoiled it.

"You know, Rudy, this better not have anything to do with that Alonzo person from yesterday," she said. "If it does, Aunt Gussie's going to cast a kitten."

"Just never mind, Hildegarde!" Rudy burst out. "It's none of your beeswax!"

He wriggled out from behind the trash can, his stomach in a knot, and headed away from the direction Danny and Vincie had taken.

"Where are you going?" Hildy Helen said. Her voice sounded bruised. "Aren't you having *lunch* with me, either?"

"No," Rudy said over his shoulder. "I'm getting my own lunch—on my bike."

And with the taste of salami already in his mouth, he ran away from her, out into the sunny, thick Chicago heat, and headed for his bike.

But the taste in his mouth turned to sawdust when he reached the wall below Little Al's office. The shiny, red bicycle from Montgomery Ward's was gone.

⁜ ⬦ ⁜

Chapter Twelve

*B*ut it had to be there. Of course—it had to.

Rudy fixed a Little-Al smirk on his face and looked around. Wouldn't it be just like Little Al to pull one of Rudy's own pranks on him and hide it someplace? Already grinning, Rudy shaded his eyes with his hand and looked up the flagpole.

But the bike wasn't hanging there with the stars and stripes. And it wasn't stashed away up on the fire escape. It wasn't even being ridden up and down Halsted Street by a devilishly grinning Little Al.

The bike was gone, and Rudy's grin disappeared, too.

"Rudolph," Aunt Gussie's crackly voice called to him from the courtyard. "Come in at once and have lunch."

When he just stood there shaking his head, she tapped the pumps across the yard with Hildy Helen at her heels. Before Aunt Gussie could start scolding, however, Hildy had her face close to Rudy's.

"What's wrong?" she said.

"He's being stubborn is what's wrong," Aunt Gussie said.

"No, something's happened. Rudy doesn't look like that unless something terrible has happened." Hildy Helen gave his arm a shake. "Rudy, talk to me!"

"My bike is gone!"

"Have you looked—" Aunt Gussie started to say.

But Hildy Helen was on her at once. "If Rudy says it's gone, it's gone. Of course he's looked for it!"

There was a moment's silence as Aunt Gussie looked from one of them to the other. Her face looked like the adding machine on Dad's desk, adding up number after number and suddenly spitting out an answer.

"All right," she said, "then let us look further for it."

They did, and so did every person on the Hull House staff Aunt Gussie could gather, along with half the members and even some people passing on Halsted Street with shopping bags over their arms. But an hour later, with lunch cold on the table in the dining hall, not a trace of the bike had been found.

"I think it's time we went home," Aunt Gussie said. Her voice wasn't as crispy as usual, and Rudy climbed into the Pierce Arrow without an argument.

"What is that horrendous smell?" Aunt Gussie said as Sol headed toward Prairie Avenue.

"Me," the old fellow said.

"Good heavens, Solomon—what have you been into?"

"Garbage."

"And why, pray tell?"

"Looking for a bike. You told me to look everywhere. I did."

Rudy suddenly felt like crying, and he glued his blurred eyes to the window.

"I'm sorry, Rudy," Hildy Helen whispered to him.

Are you? Rudy wanted to snap at her. *Even though you're on Aunt Gussie's side now?*

He didn't, though. He would hold it in until he could get back to the house and up the stairs and flat on his stomach on his bed with his sketchbook in front of him. But Quintonia met them at the door and shooed the children into the dining room for cold-cut sandwiches that Rudy didn't touch. Aunt Gussie didn't join them. She was in the library with Sol. It should have been a delightful luncheon with no one there to remind them to dab and fold and stay elbowless. But they ate in sullen silence, and as soon as Quintonia disappeared into the kitchen to fetch more lemonade, Rudy bolted for the door.

Hildy Helen was right behind him, and between her hissing, "Rudy, stop! I want to talk to you!" and Aunt Gussie emerging from the study, there was no chance of escaping to his room.

"Oh, my!" he cried out. "Look, smoke! Coming from the music room, Aunt Gussie!"

Aunt Gussie didn't even dignify his attempt with a glance over her shoulder. Instead, to his surprise, she put a hand lightly on his arm and said, "Don't worry, Rudolph. I'm not going to make you take your violin lesson today. Why don't you and Hildegarde spend the afternoon in the study? It's coolest in there."

She started off and then turned to them again. "And if you want to holler fire, try using the toaster as an excuse. Sol is convinced Quintonia is going to burn down the kitchen with it someday." Then with a nod to Sol, she disappeared into the dining room.

"Go on, then," Quintonia said and shooed them in with the books and the urns. Rudy slouched miserably into a chair. Hildy Helen slouched beside him.

"Why won't you talk to me, Rudy?" she said. "I know you're about to cast a kitten yourself. I sure would be."

"What do you care?" Rudy said. "I bet you're thinking if I'd ridden in the car like I was supposed to, it never would have happened."

Hildy Helen sat up straight in the chair, and everything on her went straight, too, from her eyebrows to her pointy chin. "Now if that isn't the biggest bunch of bushwa you have ever tried to hand me, Rudy Hutchinson, I don't know what is!"

"It's the truth!"

"It's a bold-faced lie! If you had asked me, I would have ridden my bike with you!"

"Would not!"

"You just think you know everything now—now that you're keeping company with those boys from—"

"See! You do sound like Aunt Gussie! Little Al is the swellest guy I ever met!"

"Well how would I know that? You never even introduced me to him. You never even asked me to go with you when you went to see him all those times."

"You wouldn't want to."

"Oh!" Hildy Helen folded her arms across her chest. "So you can read minds now, too?"

"Why would you want to? You're all busy with your dancing lessons and your tennis lessons and your new bathing suit."

Hildy looked at him blankly. "So?"

"So, that means you're on Aunt Gussie's side. I thought we both agreed that we were going to work on getting back to Shelbyville. No settling in here like we were gonna stay forever!"

"But Rudy," Hildy Helen said. She cocked her head curiously, as if she were just discovering something herself. "I *like* tennis and dancing and my new bathing suit. I never had any of those things in Indiana. And ever since I found out I liked them, Aunt Gussie's been different to me."

"Because she's getting her way!"

Hildy Helen shook her head. "No. I'm getting mine."

"Huh."

"Well, all except for one thing."

"Yeah, what's that, poor baby?" Rudy said. He planted his elbows firmly on the table and sunk his chin into his hands. "You still can't get your hair bobbed? Is that it?"

"No, that isn't it. It's all different between you and me," she said. "And I hate that. Do you hear me, Rudy Hutchinson? I hate it!" She stood up and gave the floor a stomp with one of her high-topped shoes. Rudy started shaking his head.

"Don't throw a tantrum, Hildy Helen, all right? I'm not in the mood for it right now."

"Well isn't that too bad! When you're in the mood to treat me like your sister again instead of some nuisance, then I guess I'll be in the mood not to have a tantrum."

Rudy looked at her doubtfully. She raised her foot threateningly above the carpet.

"All right," Rudy said. "What do you want me to do?"

"That's more like it," she said. She sat down next to him again and got her face close to his. "I want you to tell me what you think happened to your bike."

"For real?" Rudy said.

"For real."

"I think somebody stole it."

"Somebody stole it! Somebody stole it!"

They both jumped as Picasso squawked from his cage across the room.

Rudy grinned halfheartedly. "See, he thinks so, too."

"You go to Little Italy, Sol!" the bird cried. "You go to Little Italy. Find the bike! Awk! Find the bike!"

"What's he talking about?" Rudy said.

"I know exactly what he's talking about!" Hildy Helen ran across to the cage and stood on tiptoe to look nose-to-beak at Picasso.

"Is that what Aunt Gussie was saying to Sol in here?" she said.

" 'Go to Little Italy, Sol, and find the bike'?"

"Go to Little Italy. Find the bike! Don't come back without it!"

Rudy turned the chair over as he got out of it and ran to the front window. The Pierce Arrow was still parked out front. If Sol weren't going back out, he'd have put it in the garage by now, out of the blistering sun.

"All right, Hildy Helen," he said, hope rising in his chest again. "You stay here and distract Aunt Gussie. Don't let her know I've left. I'm gonna get in the car and hide and sneak to Little Italy with him."

"Nothing doing!" Hildy Helen said.

"But I thought you said you weren't on her side!"

"I'm not on her side. I'm on your side and my own side." She marched to the window. "I'm sick of being left out of things and missing all the fun. I'm going with you." She peered through the lacy curtain and gave Rudy the familiar poke. "And we'd better hurry up before Sol finishes his lunch."

"What about Quintonia?" Rudy said. "I think Aunt Gussie's got her standing guard over us or something."

Hildy Helen's face reminded him of Aunt Gussie's, working like an adding machine. Then her eyes darted to Picasso.

"I get you," Rudy said.

"Rudy's locked himself in his room," Hildy Helen said as she approached the cage. "Rudy won't come out of his room."

"Hildy Helen's in there with him," Rudy put in. "She won't come out, either."

They repeated the litany until Hildy Helen had peeked out the library door and found the upper hall empty. With their sweaty hands gripped together, they took the steps soundlessly down to the front door and slipped out. They were barely on the floor of the backseat of the long Pierce Arrow when they heard the side servants' door open. Rudy heard Hildy Helen suck in her breath.

"Don't stop breathing," he whispered. "Remember that time you did and turned blue and passed out?"

She giggled. "Hey, Rudy," she whispered. "This is fun again."

Rudy tried to concentrate on where they were as the Pierce Arrow twisted and turned through Chicago. The smells told him they were leaving the South Side's stockyards and factories and entering the West Side's groceries and restaurants. The scent of salami and garlic brought Little Al's face right into Rudy's mind.

I bet this car sticks out like a sore thumb, prowling around this neighborhood, he thought. *Little Al's gonna be alerted the minute he sees it.*

The thought suddenly tossed around in his insides. It was one he'd been trying to push aside ever since he'd realized his bike was really missing.

Hildy Helen read it as if it were words in a bubble above his head, just like in the funny papers.

"Rudy," she whispered, "you don't think your friend Al took your bike, do you?"

Rudy started to shake his head, but he couldn't.

"You do, don't you?" she whispered.

"Maybe," Rudy whispered back. And why not? That was what Little Al did, wasn't it? He went to great lengths to steal pocketbooks out of baby carriages. Why wouldn't he take a bike that was left invitingly out there in the open?

"Maybe he didn't know it was yours," Hildy Helen whispered.

Rudy was about to pooh-pooh that suggestion when suddenly the Pierce Arrow leapt forward like the head of a striking snake. With a squeal of tires, Sol took a turn and evidently jammed his foot down on the gas at the same time, because the car seemed to go up on two wheels as it rounded the corner. Hildy Helen slid against Rudy, shoving him up against the door. Before she could pull herself away, Sol careened the car in the other direction. Rudy tumbled back into Hildy Helen, pinning her to the floorboards.

She started to let out a scream as yet again Sol changed directions and sent them flying once more. Rudy managed to get his hand over her mouth and bit back his own cry. By now, Hildy Helen had her elbow in his ear and her knee right in the middle of his stomach, which, of course, was going wild on its own. There was one last heart-stopping turn, and then the Pierce Arrow lurched to a halt, throwing them into a heap Rudy was sure they'd never get untangled from. But the minute Sol threw open the driver's door and got out of the car, the twins were both up, their heads peeking over the top of the front seat.

"Where are we?" Hildy Helen whispered.

Rudy couldn't call it by name, but it was a place he'd been before, on a back street where two buildings came together. Sol had pulled up close enough to close off the triangle, and in it two figures appeared to be trapped. Sol was stomping toward them, stiff-legged and red up to the roots of his white hair.

"Is that one Al?" Hildy Helen said, pointing to the taller of the two boys.

Rudy felt a rush of relief as he shook his head. "That's Danny," he said. "And the other one's Vincie."

Hildy Helen craned her neck. "Why did Sol stop them? I don't see your bike."

Rudy didn't, either, and his heart sank. He couldn't hear what Sol was saying to the two boys, but when they scurried suddenly up a fire escape, Sol turned mechanically and headed back toward the car. Hildy Helen yanked Rudy down behind the seat with her, and both of them put fingers to their lips. Hildy Helen even screwed her eyes shut tight as Sol slowly got himself in, shut the door, and backed the Pierce Arrow out of the alley. Rudy just heard her start to breathe again when the abrupt, crusty voice said over the back of the seat, "The one with the bike got away."

Hildy Helen and Rudy stared at each other for a full minute before Rudy slowly rose up on his knees.

"How'd you know we were back here, Sol?" he said.

"Have to be deaf not to hear ya," he said.

"I thought he *was* deaf," Hildy Helen whispered.

" 'Sides," the old man added. "I'd a done the same if I was you. Sit up and help me look."

They did, both of them with eyes glued to the side windows, necks twisting like weather vanes. But there wasn't a trace of Little Al or the bike anywhere. When the shadows started to lengthen, Sol headed the car back toward Prairie Avenue, where Aunt Gussie and Dad were waiting in the library, both looking over their spectacles like a pair of judges. Rudy raised his hand and said, "I swear to tell the truth, the whole truth, and nothing but the truth—"

"Enough, Rudy," Dad said, his voice weary. "Why did you take off like that without telling anyone? Your aunt has been worried sick."

Rudy tried to grin. "I guess she didn't buy the bit about us being locked in our rooms, huh?"

"I have no idea what you're talking about," Aunt Gussie said.

Hildy Helen and Rudy looked at Picasso, who looked quite guilty, if indeed a bird can look guilty.

"Don't try to make Picasso lie for you. It won't work," Aunt Gussie said.

"Sol was cruising around in a dangerous neighborhood," Dad said. "If he'd gotten out of the car, anything could have happened to you two."

"He did," Hildy Helen said.

"And it didn't."

"Rudy," Dad said in his what-am-I-going-to-do-with-you voice.

Aunt Gussie seemed to know exactly what she was going to do with him, but just as she opened her mouth to spew it forth, the doorbell rang.

"I'll get it!" Hildy Helen cried, and Rudy started to take off after her. But Quintonia gave them a stony look from the doorway and went for the front door herself. She was back a moment later, fussing like a furious hen.

"Boy, don't you be rollin' that bicycle on these carpets! Miss Gustavia brung these back from the O-rient! She's gonna have your hide, son!"

The hide in question appeared in the study doorway, indeed wheeling a bicycle across Aunt Gussie's Oriental rugs.

"I told him not to bring that blame thing in the house!" Quintonia called over the boy's shoulder.

Little Al rolled his eyes. As if he'd ever listen to *her*.

"Rudy!" Hildy Helen cried. "That's your bike!"

"That it is. And I want to know how you came by it," Aunt Gussie said. "And don't you try to weasel your way out of this, Alonzo Delgado."

"Before anybody starts weaselin', can we get them there dirty tires off these carpets?" Quintonia said.

"Who is this young man?" Dad said, sounding more confused than anyone.

"Well, I'll tell you who he ain't."

The shouting stopped, and everyone looked at Sol.

"Who ain't—isn't—he, Sol?" Aunt Gussie said. She looked a little like a child who had just been scolded.

"He ain't the boy I seen with the bike," Sol said. "He ain't the one took it at all."

✛ ✛ ✛

Chapter Thirteen

"Well, I coulda told you that," Little Al said.

Rudy felt himself grinning to the tips of his earlobes. "Me, too!" he said. "I never thought you did it!"

Hildy Helen cleared her throat, but she didn't say anything as Rudy went straight to Little Al and stood in front of him with his hands in his pockets.

"Don't leave your belongings out in the open like that," Little Al said. "They'll steal you blind."

"Who?" Aunt Gussie said. "I want to know who is responsible for this."

Little Al looked at her as if she'd just asked him to cut off an arm. "You think I'd rat on somebody? Ain't it enough I brought it back for him?"

"Yes, it is," Dad cut in quickly. He exchanged glances with Aunt Gussie, who merely sniffed. "And we do thank you."

"Yeah, thanks," Rudy said. He shuffled his feet and waited for the grown-ups to get tired of the kids' business and go on about their own. From experience, he figured that would happen just about any second now.

"I gotta be goin'," Little Al said.

"Not without our thanking you in some way," Dad said. "At

least let us feed you some supper, eh, Auntie?" Dad turned to look at Aunt Gussie.

Rudy looked curiously at his father. Jim Hutchinson's eyes were sparkling and alert behind his rimless glasses, and his nostrils were pinched. They usually only got that way when he was working on an interesting case.

"I suppose that's the least we can do," Aunt Gussie said crisply. "Quintonia—"

But Quintonia had already gone off, still muttering to herself about the Oriental rugs.

Aunt Gussie told Sol to lock Rudy's bike up in the garage and then ushered them all into the dining room. "Come along, James," she said. "I'm sure you haven't taken the time to eat a thing all day."

Although Dad followed her dutifully into the dining room, his mind seemed to be on anything but the pork chops and applesauce and homemade raisin bread Quintonia put on the table. He only had eyes and ears, it seemed, for Little Al.

Dad sat leaning toward him during the whole meal, his food untouched on his plate, and he couldn't seem to ask enough questions. Al didn't appear to mind too much. In fact, as far as Rudy could see, he was pretty much enjoying himself.

"So tell me about your neighborhood," Dad said, and Little Al held forth for a good 15 minutes about the houses where a bunch of different families lived and the long, narrow alleys between them where all manner of dark and illegal things went on, most of which he seemed very proud of.

"Taking things off people's clotheslines does not seem to me to be a good way for a young man to spend his time," Aunt Gussie interrupted at one point. "You know Miss Jane Addams wouldn't approve."

"Yeah, well, Miss Jane Addams never had to either steal a shirt or go half naked," Little Al said matter-of-factly.

Hildy Helen and Rudy traded grins, but Dad leaned in even further. "Is that true, Al?" he said. "Have you had steal just so you wouldn't have to do without?"

Little Al shrugged. "Sometimes. But now, it's more like that's how I get ahead."

"You get ahead in this world by doing something decent with your life," Aunt Gussie said.

"You sayin' I ain't decent?" Little Al said. "What was that I done today, bringin' Rudolpho here his bicycle back?"

Hildy Helen looked at Rudy with a grin in her eyes. She was going to give him the business about *that* nickname later on, Rudy could tell. He'd have to be ready for her.

"That was very nice of you, Alonzo," Aunt Gussie was saying. "But I am talking about long term. What do you intend to do with the *rest* of your life?"

Dad cleared his throat. "Now, Auntie, if you don't mind, I'd like to concentrate on what's going on in Al's life right now. Tell me some more about your family. You say your father died?"

And then Little Al was off on another 20-minute spiel, throughout which Dad hung on every word. Rudy didn't miss any of it, either, and he knew Hildy Helen didn't, the way she stopped swirling her spoon through the applesauce to listen. Even Aunt Gussie appeared to be drawn into the story, because she didn't immediately remove the spoon and the applesauce and lecture Hildy Helen for the umpteenth time about playing with her food.

As always, Little Al drew the conversation back to the fact that *he* wasn't going to kill *himself* working on the railroads or slaving in some garment factory all his life like so many of the men in Little Italy. *He* was going to end up wearing diamond rings and sitting in the Como Inn in one of those little curtained booths, buzzing the waiter for a dinner he didn't have to worry about paying for, because there would always be somebody anxious to buy him a meal.

"If you have any sense at all," Aunt Gussie said, "you'll be like Papa Marchetti himself, the man who owns the Como Inn. He started out with a one-room café and built that restaurant into what it is today. And he never stole a cent to do it, I can guarantee you that."

She was driving her hawkish eyes into Little Al's so hard, Rudy himself was sliding down in his chair. But Little Al didn't flinch. In fact, he did everything but stand up and motion for Aunt Gussie to come on and give him more.

"Listen, Miss Gustavia," he said, "you might think you know how Papa Marchetti got his money, but you don't—not the whole story."

"Really?" Aunt Gussie said. She looked to Rudy like she was enjoying herself every bit as much as Little Al was, her mouth twitching and her eyes alive the way they got when she was listening to a radio news show. "And what makes you so sure I don't?"

"Because you ain't Italian," Little Al said simply. "What an Italian doesn't want a non-Italian to know, he won't tell, no matter what."

"Ah," Dad said. He leaned back in his chair for the first time since they'd sat down to supper. "The famous Italian Code of Silence."

"You betcha," Little Al said. He cocked his chin at Aunt Gussie. "And you can say what you want about it, Miss Gustavia, but it's saved my life more'n once."

"Nuh-uh!" Hildy Helen said. "You've never been almost killed for stealing people's wash!"

"Not for that," Little Al said, pride shining in his voice. "But I cheated death a couple times—for other things."

The "Italian Code of Silence" evidently slipped into place, because he pressed his lips together and simply wiggled his eyebrows at Hildy Helen. She wiggled hers back, but Rudy could tell she was impressed.

In fact, everybody at the table seemed to have taken a liking to Little Al, including Quintonia, who was by now leaning in the doorway listening openly to every word they were saying. Even Aunt Gussie let out a brisk, little laugh.

"I suppose I stand corrected, then, Alonzo," she said. "I fear for your life, though. Don't think you've heard the last of that from me."

"Well, I've heard the last of it for today," Little Al said. He stood up beside his chair, smeared the napkin across his face, and then stuffed it into his pocket. "I hate to eat and run, but I gotta be going."

"No need to run," Dad said. "I'll have Sol drive you. And I'll go along."

"Us, too!" Hildy Helen said.

But Dad shook his head at her and guided Little Al toward the door by the elbow. "You two have had enough adventure for today," he said. "I think I can get Little Al back home on my own."

"But not with the table linens," Quintonia said. Her eyes flashed at Little Al as she removed the linen napkin from his pocket, but Rudy could see the smile playing around her mouth.

As Dad and Little Al went out in search of Sol, Rudy watched from the dining room window. Now that his father, and maybe even Aunt Gussie, had been won over by Al's swell little self, surely Rudy wasn't going to be forbidden to hang around with him anymore. Even though half of what Little Al did was illegal, it was a good feeling to be able to be with his friend.

Rudy was still watching wistfully as the Pierce Arrow pulled out of the garage. Aunt Gussie left the dining room to go listen to the news, and Hildy Helen hurried over to him.

"Did you see that look in Dad's eye?" she said.

"When?"

"All through supper!"

"You mean that 'I'm-on-to-an-interesting-case' look? That one?"

"That's the one."

Rudy shrugged. "I guess he just likes Al. Everybody does."

"It was more than that, Rudy. And I think something important is going to happen. I haven't seen Dad look like that since we got here."

Rudy grunted. "We've barely *seen* him since we got here. He's working all the time. And when he's home, we're sleeping."

"We won't be tonight," Hildy Helen said. "I say we wait up for him and find out what he's got up his sleeve."

Hildy Helen's big brown eyes caught Rudy up in their dance. "You think?" he said.

"I know," she said.

So they pretended to wash their faces and go quietly to their rooms until the news went off and they heard Aunt Gussie go to bed. Then they planted themselves on the first landing in the shadows and waited for a man with a plan.

Sure enough, when their father came in the front door, he still had that determined walk as he hurried right into the library.

"He's making a phone call," Hildy Helen whispered.

But beyond the terse directions to the operator, they couldn't hear anything else that he was saying. Then he left the study, turned off its light, and went toward the dining room to get a snack from Quintonia, Rudy guessed. They padded soundlessly into the study themselves and looked around for clues.

"He didn't write anything down," Hildy Helen said, surveying the pad beside the telephone.

Rudy picked up the phone itself and stared into it.

"What are you doing?" Hildy Helen said. "Do you expect it to talk to you and tell you what he said?"

Rudy's eyes met hers, and Hildy Helen began to grin. Almost

in unison they burst toward the birdcage and pulled off the cover. Picasso's feathers stuck out like he'd just stuck his claw into an electrical socket. Hildy Helen put her fingers up to her lips.

"Shh!" she said to the bird.

He gave a low, hoarse croak and blinked at her.

"How do we get him to tell us what he heard?" Hildy Helen said.

Rudy thought for a minute and looked around the room. Then he snatched up a candle and held it to his ear like the phone receiver. "This is Jim Hutchinson," he said in his deepest voice.

"Awk," Picasso said, "rap sheet already. Rap sheet already!"

"What's a rap sheet?" Hildy Helen whispered.

Rudy shook his head. Picasso shook his, too. "Just the kind of kid! Just the kind of kid we've been looking for!"

"I don't know what that means," Hildy Helen said.

Rudy shrugged and flopped the cover back over the cage. "I don't think it means anything. Dad's just working on some case. He's probably forgotten all about Little Al already."

Hildy Helen crossed her arms. "I don't think so," she said.

"Well, *I'm* gonna forget about it," Rudy said.

And he did, especially because of two things that happened the very next day that sent his mind in a completely different direction. One happened just as they got to Hull House. Rudy expected the usual routine and was ready to tear off looking for Little Al in the music room where Aunt Gussie had strongly suggested he show up today. But Aunt Gussie steered them both to the front steps of Miss Jane Addams's house, where there was little foot traffic, and told them to sit down.

"Now then, Rudolph, Hildegarde," she said. "I want to know if each of you has discovered what area he or she would like to work in here at the House for the remainder of the summer."

Rudy stared at her, with what he was sure was a stupid look on his face.

"Come now, Rudolph," she said. "Surely you've had enough time to explore every nook and cranny of the place. Or have you been too busy learning the pickpocketing trade?"

Rudy felt his face turn the color of a plum, but Hildy Helen sidled in before it could go completely purple.

"I've decided," she said. "I want to work with the little girls—the ones that have the doll club and all. After all, they're going to grow up soon, and I want to help them become modern women."

"Very good," Aunt Gussie said. "So long as you don't take to bobbing everyone's hair."

She turned to Rudy, face expectant. He knew his own face was blank.

"I don't know," he said. "I didn't know that was what we were here for."

"Rudolph," she said, "the wealthy have an obligation as I see it to use what they have and what they know to help those less fortunate. That is precisely why I teach the kindergarten class for free every day."

Rudy snorted. "That's fine, Aunt Gussie. Congratulations. But in case you haven't noticed, I'm not wealthy!"

Aunt Gussie gave him an odd look. It wasn't her usual I'm-about-to-give-you-a-lecture glare or her you-are-completely-without-sense-boy face. It was a strange mixture of surprise and something else he couldn't identify. Somehow her mouth went soft and mushy, and she looked for a minute like somebody who was definitely not Aunt Gussie.

"Yes, you are wealthy, Rudolph," she said finally. "You and Hildegarde are going to inherit everything I have. Why do you think I'm grooming the two of you?"

Rudy let out a weak horse-whinny. His stomach was starting to churn, and he wasn't liking it.

"I am not joking with you," she said. Her face sprang crisply into its usual place. "I am trying to train you and Hildegarde to become people who will use the money you inherit in a way that would make the good Lord proud. Now then—" She gave her hands a generous dusting. "I want you to choose a work area by the beginning of next week."

Rudy had barely gotten over that surprise and was still wandering around Hull House in a daze at lunch time when Aunt Gussie hit him with the next one. She emerged through the front door with Little Al firmly in tow by the shoulder.

"I thought you were taking me to your *house!*" he was complaining loudly. "Not to the hoosegow!"

"What on earth would make you think I was taking you off to jail, Alonzo?" she said.

"The way you're pinching on me!" he said and shook his shoulder away.

"I'm just being cautious," Aunt Gussie said. "I know how likely you are to run away from a good thing."

Rudy and Hildy Helen looked at each other.

"What good thing?" Hildy Helen said.

"Did he say she was taking him to her house?" Rudy said. "*Our* house?"

"I did," Aunt Gussie said. "Now if you will all get into the car, Alonzo is coming home with us for the weekend."

✠ ⋅✠⋅ ✠

Chapter Fourteen

*A*s exciting as the *idea* of Little Al's spending the weekend with them was, it couldn't compare to the real thing as it unfolded. For two and a half days, Rudy kept turning to Hildy Helen and saying, "Is this real, or is it a dream?"

"Who cares?" she said to him finally. "Even if it's a dream, we'll have a lot of things to remember when we wake up!"

Friday night, Little Al got to choose whatever he wanted to do, and it was no surprise to Rudy that he picked the opera. Nor did it bother Rudy that much this time. Seeing *The Magic Flute* through Little Al's eyes—even with all those women the size of yachts warbling up there on stage—was a little like magic in itself. Although once or twice Little Al scanned the special box seats for a glimpse of his idol, Al Capone, he pretty much kept his eyes and ears on the spectacle, as if he had been enchanted by some spell.

There was pie at the Cape Cod Room in the Drake Hotel afterward. Little Al could hardly get a mouthful of apple pie a la mode into his mouth for retelling the whole story all over again, complete with a few renditions of the songs.

"I don't know how you could tell one from the other," Rudy said. "They all sounded the same to me."

"How can you say that, Rudolpho?" Little Al said.

"Because," Aunt Gussie said, looking pointedly at him and dabbing her mouth until he, too, dabbed his, "once again I have failed to find Rudolph's passion."

"I have a passion," Hildy Helen said. "Since we each get to pick something to do this weekend, I want to have my hair bobbed."

For a minute, Aunt Gussie actually seemed to be considering that. But she finally gave her head a quick little shake which reminded Rudy of Picasso and said, "And your second choice, Hildegarde?"

Hildy Helen only stuck her bottom lip out for a second before she brightened and said, "The pier!"

So the pier it was the next morning. Not only did they take Little Al on a boat excursion and introduce him to Epsicles, but he talked them into going out on the dime pier with him, where they could fish for an entire afternoon for only 10 cents. While they sat with their rented poles—and Aunt Gussie sat on the main pier with a lemonade and a bunch of old ladies who Rudy thought looked exactly like her—the three of them talked.

They discussed the best pranks they'd ever pulled, the closest they'd ever come to getting caught, and the worst thing that ever happened when they did.

"I'll tell you about our best caper," Hildy Helen said. Her brown eyes sparkled a lot like the sunlight was doing on the ripples in Lake Michigan. "Our *best* was when we put horse manure in a bag on Miss Cross Eyes's porch and set it on fire. You should have seen her trying to stomp it out!"

"We watched from the bushes," Rudy put in. "It was worth the smell just to see her jumping up and down in cow poop!"

"Did ya get caught?" Little Al said.

"No," Hildy Helen said, "and it's a good thing, or Dad would have tanned our hides for sure."

Little Al smiled around his tightened teeth. "Is that all he woulda done?"

"Isn't that enough?" Hildy Helen said.

Little Al pulled his fishing pole out of the water and waved her off with it. "If that was all I ever had to worry about if I was to get caught, I wouldn't give it a second thought. What's a little hide-tannin' against—" He stopped trying to poke a hook through a fresh worm and slowly drew his finger across his throat.

"What does that mean?" Hildy Helen said.

"It means they'd threaten him with a knife," Rudy said.

"Threaten nothin'," Little Al said. "If you get caught pullin' something against a rival gang, they don't make threats. They just bump you off."

"You mean, like, kill you?" Hildy Helen said. Her eyes were open as wide as Rudy's mouth. But she suddenly narrowed them. "I don't believe all this talk about how dangerous your pranks are, Al," she said. "I think you're just trying to impress us, don't you, Rudy?"

Rudy fumbled around for something to say, but Little Al answered first. "You can believe me or not," he said. "Ain't no skin off my nose one way or the other."

"I believe you," Rudy said quickly.

But Hildy Helen folded her arms. "I'm not so sure I do. I'd like some evidence."

Rudy groaned silently. Sometimes she just didn't know when to leave well enough alone.

Little Al swung his line back into the water and appeared to concentrate on it for a long moment, and Rudy was sure he was completely offended and would be heading back to Little Italy any minute now.

"I don't need any evidence, myself," Rudy said.

Little Al put one hand up. "It ain't like I ain't got plenty of it.

I'm startin' to play with the big boys now a little, you know."

"What big boys?" Hildy Helen asked.

"I'm talkin' about the mob, see. I try to make myself available, just in case they need an errand run or somethin'. Gotta let 'em know I can be trusted. Let 'em get to know my face, that kinda thing."

"Yeah, and?" Hildy Helen said.

Little Al narrowed his eyes at her from under his cap. "You ever heard of Baby Joe Esposito?"

The name ran through Rudy's head like a question on a history test. He knew the answer, but it was just out of his reach.

"Who's that? Somebody's little brother?" Hildy Helen said.

Little Al gave another sneer. "For people with a lotta dough, you sure don't know what's goin' on in the world."

Rudy squirmed on the pole he was perched on. He sure wished Hildy Helen would just let it go.

"Baby Joe Esposito was Big Tim Murphy's right-hand man," Little Al said.

"Oh, that explains it," Hildy Helen said. She rolled her eyes.

"I happen to know from somebody who sometimes hangs out with one of the Boss's rod men—"

"What's a 'rod man'?" Hildy Helen asked.

"A guy who carries a rod—a gun."

"Oh," Hildy Helen said. The challenging sparkle disappeared from her eyes.

Little Al took a final, patient stab at his story. "This guy tol' me that the Boss has got it in for anybody associated with Big Tim Murphy. So I took it on myself to start followin' Baby Joe whenever I could, just in case I could be useful in some way." He smiled through his teeth. "And I was."

He continued to fish as if that were all that needed to be said.

It wasn't enough for Hildy Helen. "How?" she said.

"Let's just say I was at the right place at the right time," Little

Al said. "And I tol' somebody somethin' they needed to know. I was the mouse, see? And that led to Baby Joe bein'—"

Al suddenly seemed to catch himself, as if he'd spit out something he couldn't get back into his mouth.

"Go on," Hildy Helen said.

Al shook his head. "It's too dangerous, see?" he said. "I almost got plugged myself at the time."

"Plugged?" Hildy Helen said.

Rudy's stomach was starting to churn. Somehow, he didn't really want to know what "plugged" meant.

"Shot fulla holes," Little Al said simply. "Don't you ever listen to the radio? You don't know nothin'."

But at the moment, Rudy knew enough. He remembered with a chill that froze his churning stomach exactly where he'd heard the name Baby Joe Esposito before. Because he *had* listened to the radio. A shadow fell across Rudy's weekend.

It didn't stay for long. After they'd caught enough fish for the next morning's breakfast, they went back to the main pier where the action was just starting for the evening in the big ballroom at the end. Aunt Gussie let them stand on tiptoe and peer through the window at the dancers, and Rudy thought Hildy Helen would come right out of her skin.

"They're doing the Charleston again!" she squealed. "I'd *die* to know how to Charleston."

Aunt Gussie told her a well-bred young woman didn't need to know how to Charleston, but she certainly needed to know how to waltz. When Little Al chimed in that he wouldn't mind learning how to waltz, seeing how "dames love a guy who can waltz," Aunt Gussie taught the two of them right there on the pier, with Rudy looking on and guffawing and mocking them every box step of the way.

It was getting dark by the time they left the pier and headed back to Prairie Avenue. Aunt Gussie said, "It's your turn,

Rudolph. What is your pleasure for the evening?"

That was one question Rudy did know the answer to, but he just took off his cap and shook out his curls.

"What does that mean?" she said.

"I know what I want to do," he said. "But you'll never let us. You think it's a third-base art something or other."

"What on earth are you talking about?"

"I want to see a movie," Rudy said. "I never seen one, only posters. But you said you think film is a—"

"Debased art form," Aunt Gussie said.

"Yeah, that was it."

"I never said anything of the kind."

"Yes, you did that day all those old ladies were over at the house."

"The Women's War Economy League," inserted Hildy Helen.

"What you *heard* while you were *eavesdropping*," Aunt Gussie said, drilling her eyes into Rudy, "was my fellow league members saying film was a debased art form. I never said anything of the kind."

"But you didn't tell them they were wrong!" Rudy said.

"How could I? I've never seen a moving picture myself, and I've been meaning to." She leaned up to the front seat. "Solomon," she instructed, "directly after supper we shall need for you to take us to the Biograph Theater."

Rudy grinned, but he couldn't help stealing a curious glance at Aunt Gussie. He had to admit it: He just couldn't figure her out.

That evening was the best part of the weekend dream for Rudy—seeing Laurel and Hardy, the tall, thin comedian and his wide, mustached friend running into each other and making bizarre faces on the flickering screen. Rudy was spellbound by their antics, all performed by some miracle in a darkened movie theater that was itself splendid with red velvet hangings and plush seats to match. He was as enthralled with it all as Al had been with the opera. Aunt Gussie seemed to be pretty thrilled by it, too, because the next day she made a surprise announcement.

They went to church, of course, and to Sunday school. They were studying about how Jesus made time to let all the kids sit on His lap. It was about the 40th time Hildy Helen and Rudy had heard it. Rudy busied himself by drawing a rakish picture of Jesus with Little Al, Hildy Helen, Danny, and Vincie on His lap—Little Al picking the Lord's pocket, Danny trying to make off with His crown of thorns, and Vincie busily bobbing Hildy Helen's hair for her. When the Sunday school teacher—another old lady who looked just like Aunt Gussie except that her hair had a strange bluish tinge—had Hildy Helen stand up and recite the Bible verse they were supposed to have learned, Rudy held up the drawing so she'd have the urge to giggle. It paid off. Every time she got to "whosoever shall receive this child in my name," she let out a guffaw and had to start over.

Meanwhile, Little Al chafed against the collar of the new, stiff shirt Aunt Gussie had bought him. He looked as if he would rather be raiding trash cans in a Little Italy alley than spend one more moment in a church. Rudy looked nervously at the big wall clock. If this boring stuff didn't end soon, Little Al was going to make a break for it, Rudy could tell.

Even as Rudy was looking longingly at the door, Aunt Gussie herself appeared, and Miss Blue Hair wound up the class. Still afraid that Little Al might climb out the nearest window, Rudy grabbed his arm and said, "I think we can go now."

Miss Blue Hair got to Aunt Gussie first, and Hildy Helen took hold of Rudy's other arm.

"I bet she's going to tell her I couldn't get through my Bible verse," she whispered. "There goes the rest of the weekend for me."

"Gustavia," Miss Blue Hair said in a voice shrill as a piccolo, "where were you at the Women's War Economy League meeting on Friday?"

"Not there, obviously," Aunt Gussie said.

Hildy Helen poked Rudy. This ought to be good, seeing Aunt Gussie get scolded for once.

"I could *see* that," said Miss Blue Hair. "And why weren't you?"

Aunt Gussie's eyes never wavered. "I've decided the League is no longer for me."

Miss Blue Hair let out a gasp so loud you'd have thought she'd just been "plugged." "How can you say that when you know what we stand for?" she cried, her hand against her chest.

"It's because I've finally discovered what you stand for that I want out," Aunt Gussie said.

"You don't think we should stand up against liquor and cigarettes?"

"It's the standing up against jewelry and parties in the home I couldn't quite agree with," Aunt Gussie said.

"People do not need those things," Miss Blue Hair said, drawing herself up until she resembled a blue-leaded pencil. "Fancy clothes and other useless ornaments—"

"Oh, for crying out loud, Mildred," Aunt Gussie said. "I would much rather use my energies against things that might actually hurt someone. I see absolutely no harm in beauty or fun."

Miss Blue Hair clutched harder at the front of her blouse. "The next thing you know, you'll be going to the moving pictures!"

Hildy Helen and Rudy nudged each other.

"To tell you the truth, Mildred," Aunt Gussie said, "I already have, and I was mesmerized. In fact, I'm taking the children back this afternoon. We're going to see *King of Kings* at the Chicago Theater."

"You'll be sorry you did this, Gustavia," were Miss Blue Hair's parting words. "Putting the life of Jesus on that brazen screen is blasphemy."

"I'll take my chances," Aunt Gussie said dryly.

Little Al dove forward. "Let me get that door for ya, Miss Gustavia," he said.

"To what do I owe this sudden rush of good manners?" she said.

Little Al gave his tight grin. "I like an old doll like you," he said.

"Thank you," she said.

The old doll took them to the Chicago Theater, which was even fancier than the Biograph, and Rudy was so wrapped up in gazing at the crystal chandeliers and gold leaf ceiling that he forgot Miss Blue Hair had said the film was about the life of Jesus until the lights went down and CECIL B. DEMILLE PRESENTS *King of Kings* flickered up onto the screen.

It doesn't matter, Rudy thought. *I'm sure it won't be that boring. It's the movies after all.*

As it turned out, there wasn't a boring moment in it. From the very beginning, with the silent scenes and their words flashing up every now and then, Rudy felt like he was watching a movie about today. Herod's town was like the streets of Chicago: Not a day went by without a murder and one ordered by a mob leader at that. The people were all partying and carousing, just like the flappers and their boyfriends the kids had seen in the ballroom, and all anybody seemed to care about was money. In different costumes, with a few skyscrapers and a Model A or two, it might have been Chicago in 1928.

And then came Jesus. *Here we go*, Rudy thought. *Mr. Milquetoast comes in and stops all the fun.*

But Jesus was no Caspar Milquetoast. In fact, within the first 10 minutes, he replaced Tom Mix as Rudy's favorite film hero. He got right up into the faces of the pointy-nosed scribes and Phar-

isees and made them look like saps; He convinced the people who
were down on their luck that they were just as good as everybody
else; and He popped everybody's eyes out with those stunts he
pulled, turning the loaves and fishes into a big banquet and all.

Rudy had heard about it all a hundred times in Sunday school,
but it had never occurred to him until he saw Jesus up there
walking around that He had actually been a person—and a swell
one at that.

"Well, Rudolph," Aunt Gussie said when they were back in the
Pierce Arrow, "I don't suppose Jesus was too dull for you?"

"Are you kidding?" Rudy said.

"He sure pulled off some capers with that Pharisino gang,
didn't he?" Little Al said.

"Something like that," Aunt Gussie said. "He was a man of
great passion, and He never settled for doing things the way they
had always been done." She slanted her eyes toward Rudy from
under her gray cloche hat. "He reminded me somewhat of you,
Rudolph."

Hildy Helen nearly choked.

"The biggest difference between Rudolph and Jesus," Aunt
Gussie said, giving Hildy Helen a hard look, "is that your brother
has not yet found his passion so that he can use it for good." Her
eyes went back to Rudy. "You will notice that while Jesus was
outlandish, as you are, He never used that simply to show off or
to hide something."

Rudy couldn't hold her eyes any more. He looked casually out
the window and watched Chicago slip off into its summer twi-
light. He needed to find his passion so he wouldn't have to show
off or hide things. The way Jesus did.

What did all of that mean?

If it had been an emergency, he knew he would have prayed
about it.

✠ ⚬✠⚬ ✠

Chapter Fifteen

*T*hey wound up the weekend at the railroad yard, where they played hide and seek. Then they perched on an abandoned railroad trestle and swung their legs over the brick-lined alley below. Rudy could see Little Al automatically reaching into his pocket. It really was the perfect time for chewing on a couple of hunks of salami.

"Wish we had some cigarettes," Little Al said. "If I was in my own part of town I'd just steal myself some."

"Why?" Hildy Helen said.

"Because they cost 10 cents a pack! You think I got that to spend on Camels?"

Hildy Helen folded her arms. "I wish you wouldn't steal."

"Look, I heard that song enough times, ain't you, Rudy?"

Rudy looked down at his hands. "Sure," he said.

"See, it's different when you're part of the action," Little Al said. He leaned toward Hildy Helen. "You oughta pull a caper with us one time. You're a smart doll—you'd be good at it."

"Us?" Hildy Helen said.

Her brown eyes widened, and she turned slowly to Rudy. He looked back at her and shrugged.

"Rudy, he's my stall. He needs more practice, but he'll get the hang of it. You could be my shade."

"What's a shade?" Rudy said, turning deliberately away from Hildy Helen.

"Like my assistant," Little Al said. He cocked his mouth to one side and wiggled his eyebrows at Hildy Helen. "You'd protect me, see."

"From what?" Hildy Helen said.

"From gettin' caught." He puffed out his little chest. "'Course, gettin' caught by a squad of bulls ain't no big deal. Not like bein' nabbed by a gang."

Both Hildy Helen and Rudy were looking at him blankly.

"Squad of bulls?" Hildy Helen said.

Little Al threw up his hands. "I forgot you two ain't hip. Squad of bulls—that's the police. All's you get is yer name on a rap sheet and they let ya go."

A bell went off in Rudy's head, and he could tell the same one was jangling inside Hildy Helen's brain.

"So, whaddya say?" Little Al said to her. "Are you in?"

"I don't think so," she said.

"Well, now that I've told her my game, I'm gonna have to kill her," Little Al said to Rudy. "She knows too much."

"What?" Hildy Helen said.

Little Al jerked his chin up and laughed a tight laugh. "Just foolin' with ya. They only do that in the big time. Me, I'm small potatoes. But I won't be forever after what I done about Baby Joe, you can bet on that."

Rudy didn't want to. He didn't even want to think about it. Somehow, the "thrill of the underworld" had fizzled for him. He wished it would fizzle for Little Al, too.

On the contrary, Little Al suddenly sat up straight on the trestle and put his finger to his lips. His eyes darted first one way, then the other, while his head barely moved.

"What? What is it?" Hildy Helen said.

Little Al cut her off with a glance and slowly inched his way down the trestle until he could just see down into the dark alley below. Hildy Helen looked at Rudy, her face a question mark, but he shrugged and stretched his neck to try and see what Little Al was gazing at.

Whatever it was, it brought the little Italian up with a jerk.

"Gotta go," he hissed to them. "You oughta make tracks for home, too."

Before even Hildy Helen could get a question out, he made for one of the iron legs of the trestle and scrambled down it like a monkey. Seconds later, his head came back up and he whispered, "Tell Miss Gustavia thanks for everything." And then he was gone again.

Rudy started to wriggle down the trestle the way Little Al had, but once he was away from the wall and hanging out over bare space, he felt his palms get sweaty.

"Come back, Rudy," Hildy Helen called to him. "If you fall and kill yourself, I'll never forgive you!"

"Now ain't that sweet?"

The voice seemed to come out of nowhere, and Hildy Helen and Rudy whirled toward it. Not 10 feet beyond where Rudy had gotten to was the outline of a man in a fedora, silhouetted against the murky-dark sky. Rudy couldn't see his face, and he was pretty sure that was just the way the man wanted it.

"Who are you?" Hildy Helen said.

Rudy almost groaned out loud. What difference did it make who he was? He looked so sinister standing there straddling the bridge with his arms folded and his face shaded, Rudy would have run from him if he were the pastor of the Methodist church.

"I'll ask the questions," the man said. His voice was no longer sarcastic. It had the sound of nails being shaken around in a tin bucket, and every one of them went through Rudy.

"You seen a kid?" the man said.

Rudy tried to grin, and he pointed at Hildy Helen. "Right there," he said.

"I'm talkin' about a boy kid, smart guy. You seen one—'round this height?" He stuck out his hand about four feet from the ground. "Little tough guy."

"No!" Rudy said before Hildy Helen could start squealing. Then he grinned again. "Who'd be crazy enough to be climbing around on this thing, huh?"

In two strides the man was on him, his hand clutching the front of Rudy's shirt and bringing him to a stand-up right in his face. Even that close, Rudy couldn't make out a single feature. He was too busy gasping for air. One step off balance and they'd both go crashing to the bricks below.

"Don't give me the business, kid, or I'll give you the back of my hand, y'see?"

"How could I help but see?" Rudy said in a whisper. "You're two inches away."

The man gave him a shake, and the last of the jokes tumbled out of Rudy. He grabbed on to the first thing he could find—the man's arms. They were like two steel bands.

"I haven't seen anybody!" he cried. "Honest, mister!"

"He hasn't! If he had, I'd have seen him, too, and I didn't. Let him go!"

Hildy Helen's voice had gone strident as a flute, but it seemed to do the job, because the man let go of Rudy's shirt abruptly. Struggling for his balance, Rudy grabbed for the man again, his hands flying out like startled chickens. One of them brushed against the velvety brim of the fedora and sent it toppling off the back of the man's head.

He turned with a jerk, snatched it up, and smashed it back over his hair, but not before Rudy caught the only glimpse of his face he got. All he saw were the stranger's glinting eyes. The man pointed them over his shoulder at Rudy.

"Go on, get outta here!" he said. "The botha youse. Kids like you don't belong here anyways. Go back to your rich mommy and daddy!"

Rudy would have gone to the moon if the man had told him to. Scrambling like a chased spider, he reached Hildy Helen, and the two of them jumped the few feet from the trestle to the wall and didn't stop running until they were almost to Prairie Avenue. Neither one of them dared look back, but the sound of footsteps never echoed behind them.

When they got to the house, Rudy threw himself against the corner wall and grabbed himself around the middle. Hildy Helen flopped down on the ground.

"I've never been so scared in my life, Rudy!" she said. "You were scared, too. You were."

Rudy didn't deny it. He knew his face was pasty white. All he wanted to do was sit here until his heart stopped trying to pound its way out of his chest.

"You know he was talking about Little Al, don't you?" Hildy Helen said.

Rudy nodded.

"That man must have been who Al saw when he was looking down from the trestle," she said.

"Uh-huh."

"You don't think he'll find him, do you? Do you think he was a bull? Or do you think he was a gang person? I mean, that would make the difference between whether Al got plugged or—"

Rudy found himself staring at her. She started to grin.

"I sound hip, don't I?" she said. And then she shook the strings of dark hair out of her face. "But that isn't the point. Little Al could be in big trouble."

"I think Little Al *stays* in big trouble," Rudy said.

"You aren't going to keep being his stall, or whatever you call it, are you Rudy?"

"Are you kiddin'?" he said. "You didn't feel that guy's arms. I thought he was gonna throw me off the bridge! And from the sound of his voice, I think he was the one who shot Baby Joe Esposito at the train station."

"Well, if he was a policeman," Hildy Helen said, "then you'd just get a rap sheet, although I don't know what for—"

"Rap sheet," Rudy said. "Isn't that what Picasso said the other night when he was telling us what Dad was talking about on the phone?"

"Yeah. 'Already has a rap sheet.' "

"You think it was Little Al he was talking about? You know, when he was saying 'just the kind of kid we've been looking for'?"

Hildy Helen considered that and then shook her head. "I don't think so. Dad likes Little Al. He wouldn't try to finger him."

"What does *that* mean?" Rudy said.

Hildy Helen smiled proudly. "Finger? Oh, that means when you turn somebody in to the police. Little Al taught me that."

"Oh," Rudy said. "Then you're right. Dad must have been talking about somebody else."

"Still." Hildy Helen folded her arms. "I just wish Little Al would quit stealing. Especially if he has people like that running after him."

"Yeah," Rudy said.

"But what I don't understand is, if that man was one of Al Capone's, and Little Al was helping Al Capone, why would one of his men be after Little Al?"

"To thank him?" Rudy said.

He tried to grin at Hildy Helen, but she didn't grin back. Together they went gloomily into the house. The weekend ended in the shadows.

But the week held more promise. Little Al showed up at Hull House the next day all in one piece, and when the twins asked him if the man who'd been chasing him had caught him, he looked at them in his tight, little, crooked way and said, "Bushwa!" When they filled him in on their encounter with the dark man, Little Al patted Rudy's shoulder and said, "Ya done good, kid. I'm tellin' ya—ya got a future in the underworld."

There was no more talk of the mob or the thrilling life of a criminal that day, however, or for several days afterward. After lunch, Aunt Gussie invited Little Al to come home with them for the afternoon, and she did the same thing every day for the rest of the week.

"I told you I like an old doll like you," Little Al said to her that first day as Sol cruised the Pierce Arrow back to Prairie Avenue. "You sure know how to treat a fella."

It became obvious to Rudy right away that Aunt Gussie had more in mind than treating Little Al to a good time.

"Rudolph," she said on Monday when it was time for Rudy to scratch and squeal the bow for Leo, "I'm going to ask you to do something unselfish."

"He'll do it," Little Al said, punching Rudy good-naturedly on the arm. "He's a prince among men, this one."

"That's a bit of an exaggeration, Alonzo, but I think Rudolph will be completely generous in this case." She turned to Rudy, who was by now thinking the worst. "Would you consider giving up your violin lessons and allowing Alonzo to have them instead?"

Rudy couldn't answer her fast enough. He even escorted Al to the music room, introduced him to Leo with perfect manners, and stuck a bow in the kid's hand before his great aunt had a chance to change her mind.

Of course, he couldn't resist standing outside the music room door with Hildy Helen, waiting to chortle over the horrible noises Little Al was bound to make on his first try. As it turned out, the little Italian had, as Leo put it over and over again, "A gift! You have a gift, my child. Mwa! Mwa! Mwa!"

"What is he doing?" Hildy Helen whispered.

Little Al revealed that when he emerged from the music room. "The lesson was swell," he said to them. "But I coulda done without all the kissin' on the cheeks."

And so they fell into a routine. Every day after lunch at Hull House, they all piled into the Pierce Arrow and went home, where Little Al had his lesson and the twins spent their hour in the study. Then they tore off for adventures in the backyard. They even found a tunnel in the stone wall they could crawl through to the street. It was a smaller world than Little Al was used to, but it seemed to be different enough to hold his attention. Dad started coming home for supper every night, and the conversation always turned to Little Al and his past.

"Tell me more about your father," Dad said on Thursday.

"Nothin' more to tell," Little Al said.

Rudy chewed thoughtfully on his steak and watched his friend. Al had suddenly taken an unusual interest in lining up his pieces of potato on his plate.

"What did you say he died of?" Dad said.

"I didn't," Al said. He scooted a square of spud a fraction of an inch over.

"Ah," Dad said. "I'm sorry. I'm prying."

Little Al grinned back a little too fast. "Nah, you ain't pryin'. I ain't afraid to talk about it. He had—they said—well, it was somethin' to do with his liver or somethin' like that. You know them doctors. They talk Greek or somethin'. All's I know is, he just up and died."

"Al," Dad said it so softly, Rudy wasn't sure he heard it, "I think you know exactly what happened to your father. He died of alcohol poisoning, didn't he?"

"Maybe it was somethin' like that." The potatoes were in a line straight as a ruler, and there was nothing left for Little Al to do. He stared at the table.

"And you know where he got it, too, don't you?" Dad said.

"Dad," Hildy Helen said. "You're making Little Al feel bad."

"Nah, I'm all right," Little Al said. "It ain't no secret my old man drank bootleg whiskey. I mean, who don't, what with liquor bein' against the law? The only pure stuff you get's from Canada—"

"Bootleg whiskey—made by bootleggers, careless ones. Mobsters, Al."

"They didn't do it on purpose, though!" Al said. "Accidents happen!"

"They wouldn't happen if the mob didn't—"

"You ain't sayin' Al Capone killed my old man, are ya, Mister Hutchie? 'Cause if that's what you're sayin', well, I think I oughta be goin'."

Rudy whirled on his father, but Dad was already shaking his head. "No, no, I'm not accusing anybody in particular. Let's drop it for now, shall we?"

"I wish we'd never brought it up in the first place," Hildy Helen said primly. Then she dabbed at her mouth with her napkin.

Once again, the subject of the crime world was dropped—until the very next night, Friday, when Little Al moved in for the weekend again and Judge Caduff appeared for dinner.

As soon as he gave Rudy his hand-crushing handshake when he arrived at the table, Rudy remembered that he kind of liked the big ex-boxer. Little Al was more suspicious.

"Yer a lawman, huh?" Little Al said.

Judge Caduff's blue eyes twinkled. "I like to think so."

"Huh."

"You don't like lawmen?"

"Not much," Little Al said and began casually attacking his apple salad.

"Alonzo, really—" Aunt Gussie started to say.

But Judge Caduff shook his head at her. "It's all right, Gussie," he said. "I like honesty."

Al looked openly at the judge while he crunched his apples.

"So why is that?" Judge Caduff said.

" 'Cause you fellas ain't always fair. Always puttin' people away that ain't done nothin' wrong."

The ex-boxer folded his beefy hands in front of his plate. "For example?" he said.

"Right off the bat, when Al Capone first come here from New York," Al said, "the law tried to send him up the river for an automobile accident, something that coulda happened to anybody! Then—"

"Now wait just a minute," the judge said. His voice was patient, and his face wreathed into a knowing smile. "First of all, Mr. Capone was drunk at the time, and he was driving at a high rate of speed. And when he crashed into the taxicab, which, I might add, was simply parked at the curb, Mr. Capone got out of his car and pointed a gun at the taxi driver."

"He thought he was one of his rivals trying to kill him!" Little Al said.

"Oh," Judge Caduff said. He laughed his wonderful, wheezy laugh. "And that makes it all right."

"The thing is, the police and the resta you fellas oughta stay out of family business. That's what it is, y'know. The Italians are all a family."

"So, we should stay out of it while your 'family' runs down innocent people on the streets and points pistols at whomever they please?"

Rudy set down his fork beside his unfinished canned green beans. All of this was making him lose his appetite. Of course, the judge was right, but was he *trying* to run Little Al right out of there?

"It was a case of mistaken identity that time," Little Al said.

"Most of the time, we can settle our own differences. We don't need police or judges."

The judge leaned forward until his big chest pressed the table-cloth. "Then how, Al, do you explain the fact that Mr. Capone was wearing a special deputy sheriff's badge at the time, and he displayed it while he was threatening to shoot the cab driver?"

Little Al looked for once as if he didn't have an answer, but slowly a tight grin started to appear on the little Italian's face.

"He done that?" he said.

"Yes, he did," said the judge.

"See how smart he is!" Little Al cried.

"Yes, I do. He was even smart enough to get himself out of the whole mess and never did a day of jail time for it. And it's unfortunate to me that a man clever and charming enough to do all of that wouldn't use his gifts for good instead."

"He ain't never killed nobody," Little Al said, his face set stubbornly. "You fellas ain't never proved he killed nobody."

Judge Caduff sighed. "You're right about that. Mr. Capone still walks around Chicago as if he owned it."

There was an uneasiness at the table as they all returned to their plates and continued to eat in silence. Rudy groped for something funny to say—for *anything* to say. But all he could do was wish the judge had never brought any of this up in the first place. It was Little Al himself who burst into the quiet.

"I'll say one thing for ya, though, Judge," he said, waving his bean-filled fork for effect.

"What's that?" Judge Caduff said.

"You know how to show respect. I appreciate you callin' him Mr. Capone, 'stead of Scarface and all them other names the newspaper is always shoutin' out."

Judge Caduff threw back his massive head and wheezed out a laugh. Everyone else joined in, including Rudy. Although for the life of him, he couldn't figure out why.

✢ ✢ ✢

Chapter Sixteen

*R*udy was glad that Judge Caduff didn't come back for the rest of the weekend. Aunt Gussie took the children to the movies to see *Lights of New York,* the first talking picture with sound all the way through. Then they went to the opera, where Little Al cried through most of *La Traviata.* Afterward, she also taught them all how to play mah-jongg, the newest game craze. After that, Hildy Helen was convinced she was "modern" now, although she still whined about wanting her hair bobbed.

But Rudy couldn't be distracted from thinking back to that dinner table conversation with Judge Caduff. After listening to the big boxer talk about Al Capone, Rudy was ready to go after the gangster himself and get him off the streets. But Little Al hadn't even been swayed, much less knocked away from his dream of following in the Boss's footsteps, and that made Rudy's stomach churn.

On Sunday night after Dad had taken Little Al home, Rudy waited up for his father in the study. Dad looked as if he were ready to pick up his briefcase and work half the night, but when his eyes brushed over Rudy, folded stiffly into a leather chair, he set his case down and took a chair beside his son.

"You're looking pensive," Dad said.

"What's that mean?" Rudy said.

"It means you're having some deep thoughts that aren't necessarily making you happy." He reached out a long-fingered hand and ran it through Rudy's curls. "Not the usual thing for you, I'd say. I have half a mind to look over my shoulder to see what kind of prank you and your sister have brewing." He smiled his faint smile. "Am I being set up?"

Rudy shook his head, and Dad's smile faded. "What is it, son?" he said.

"What would happen to Little Al if he got caught doing something really bad?" Rudy blurted out. "Would he go to prison?"

Dad sighed all the way from his toes. "I'm afraid he would, Rudy. That's just what Judge Caduff and I are working on. We'd like to see the system return to what your grandfather started here—where juveniles would have their own facility, where they would be rehabilitated instead of going to adult prisons."

"I don't know what rehabobulated means."

"Changed for the better," Dad said. "The other thing to do, of course, is to keep him from doing something really bad in the first place. You know that's one of the reasons your aunt keeps inviting him to stay here."

"Yeah, I knew that," Rudy said.

"Do you think it's working?"

Rudy looked down at the table. Should he tell Dad what Little Al had hinted at that day when he and Hildy Helen and Rudy were fishing? Should he let him know that Little Al had probably already done something bad—bad enough, he knew now, to send him off to prison?

Dad said, "We're doing all we can for him, son. Be his friend, not just someone who goes along with everything he does. Do you understand that?"

Rudy nodded miserably. That was a whole lot easier to say than to do.

The focus stayed on Little Al, like always, until the next day when Aunt Gussie, Hildy Helen, and Rudy were on their way back to Hull House.

"Rudolph," Aunt Gussie said, "have you decided which area you want to work in for the rest of the summer? Your deadline is approaching." She sniffed and brushed some lint off her skirt.

"Yeah," Rudy said.

She looked up in surprise.

"I want to work in the art class—help teach the little kids."

"Art class?" she said.

"Oh, yeah, why didn't I think of that?" Hildy Helen said. "Rudy's a great artist, Aunt Gussie. He draws some funny pictures—"

With a look from Rudy, Hildy Helen clapped her hands over her mouth. Aunt Gussie looked from one of them to the other. Hildy Helen, Rudy decided, was definitely going to get it for opening her mouth this time. All he needed was for Aunt Gussie to get a load of some of the cartoons he'd drawn of her.

"Well, this is news," Aunt Gussie said. "Show me your work this afternoon."

"I'm sorry, Rudy," Hildy Helen whispered to him as they scurried off down one of the halls together a few minutes later. "But you'll have time to hide the ones that could get you in trouble before she looks at them."

"I don't get why she even has to see them," Rudy muttered. "You didn't have to give proof when you decided where you wanted to work."

When they got home that afternoon and Little Al was bowing away at "Three Blind Mice" in the music room with Leo, Rudy raced up to his room to hide his drawings of Aunt Gussie, while Hildy Helen stalled her downstairs. He finally had them stuffed safely into his pillowcase and was headed toward the door with the rest of them in a folder when Aunt Gussie rapped sharply and stuck her head in. Rudy froze. It seemed to him that Aunt Gussie's eyes went right for the bed.

"I've got the drawings right here," Rudy said. "Want to look at them in the library?" He gave her his most charming grin. "I'll race you down the banister."

Her eyes squinted behind her glasses. "No, right here will be fine. Since I came all the way up here, I might as well stay."

She swept past him, her pumps as always tapping the hardwood floor, and placed herself primly next to a stiff-cushioned chair Rudy used for a second closet. It was currently covered with the clothes he'd worn to Hull House yesterday.

"Rudolph," she said, "just because we have servants does not give you license to live like a pig. Kindly remove these clothes."

Rudy picked them up in one big ball and deposited them into the bottom of the armoire. When he turned back, Aunt Gussie was sitting in the chair, shaking her head.

"Sometimes I think I'll have better luck training Alonzo than you," she said. "And I want to warn you, I am not going to allow you to work in the art area at Hull House if you think it's going to be playtime. Stick figures cavorting across the page is not art, no matter how 'funny' it may be."

Rudy felt his fingers tighten around his folder of drawings. He suddenly didn't want to show them to her at all. He'd rather work in the kitchen peeling potatoes than let her see his artwork if that was the way she was going to be.

But no smart comebacks jumped into his head. In fact, his stomach churned, and he realized he was a little sad. Just when he'd thought she might not be such an old bag after all, she started acting like one again.

"Well?" she said. "Shall we have a look?"

"Nah, never mind," Rudy said. "They're just stick figures, like you said."

"Rudolph," she said, her hand held out, "the drawings, please."

Feeling as if he were peeling off his skin, Rudy let go of them and stuck the folder into her hand. Then he went to the bed and flopped down on it with his hands behind his head on the pillow, just in case she decided to search the room next. He stared up at the ceiling and felt lost again. He hadn't felt that way since—well, since Little Al had started coming home with them.

Huh, home, he thought. *This isn't any more home than it ever was—not with her.*

"Rudolph," Aunt Gussie said.

Rudy struggled up onto one elbow and looked at her.

"Do you know what you have done here?" she said.

"I thought I was drawing pictures," Rudy said. "Silly me, huh?"

"You have done caricature."

"I sure didn't mean to," Rudy said. "I don't even know what that is."

"The artist focuses on a person's most outstanding feature, often his or her most comical, and draws a portrait in which that feature is larger than life."

"I never did that," Rudy said.

"Yes, you did, and quite well, I have to say. That's the beauty of it. You did it without thinking."

"I don't think so," Rudy said. But he was sitting all the way up now.

"Come here and see," she said.

Rudy scrambled off the bed to look at his drawing of Judge Caduff standing in the boxing ring in his robe.

"What catches your eye about this man in the drawing right away?" Aunt Gussie said.

"His hands," Rudy said. "They're big."

"Indeed they are. It's quite clever actually, what you've done."

Rudy wasn't sure, but he thought he heard her chuckle. "They are all quite witty and original, and I must admit, you show talent. You are a promising cartoonist, Rudolph."

"You mean, like those fellas that draw Mickey Mouse?"

"I suppose."

"That's a bunch of applesauce, Aunt Gussie," Rudy said. "You're just saying that because I'm your great-nephew."

"Rudolph, you are smarter than that. Nothing but an honest opinion ever comes out of my mouth."

He knew that about Aunt Gussie. But talent? Him? For anything besides playing pranks? It was a little hard to swallow.

"Now this one," she said, "I'm a little concerned about."

She produced the drawing of Jesus with the twins and Little Al on His lap. Rudy fiddled with the curls on his forehead and tried to smile. "That's a good one, eh?"

"Artistically speaking, yes," she said. "It's one of your better ones, in fact. But it borders on disrespect for the Lord, do you see that?"

"I was just joking around," Rudy said.

"I think God has a sense of humor," Aunt Gussie said. "Otherwise, why would He have created the rhinoceros? But to poke fun at His Son—I'm not so sure that would tickle His funny bone."

"Sorry," Rudy mumbled.

"I think we can remedy that in short order. I want you to begin to get to know Jesus, Rudolph."

"Bring him in. We'll have a peanut butter and jelly sandwich together. I haven't had one since we've been here. Quintonia says that's poor folks' food or something."

"Rudolph, be serious for an instant, would you please?"

"Sure," Rudy said. "But no longer than that."

"I think you began to understand Him when we saw *King of Kings*. Since then I've watched you waver back and forth between wanting to be like Him and wanting to be twins with Little Al.

You've studied Little Al until you know him inside out. Now I want you to do the same with Jesus. I think something surprising is going to happen as a result."

"Didn't you watch the end of that movie, Aunt Gussie?" Rudy said. "Jesus isn't around right now. How am I supposed to get to know Him?"

"Draw Him," Aunt Gussie said. "Listen in church and Sunday school, observe, and then draw. I'd like to see your drawings Monday morning."

With that she tucked the sketches neatly back into the folder and handed it to him. "There's one more thing, Rudolph," she said as she walked toward the door.

"What's that?" Rudy said.

"There was one person I didn't see any drawings of. Me."

✞-✞-✞

Chapter Seventeen

*W*orking with the younger children in their art classes turned out to be more fun than Rudy would have guessed. The children seemed to like having him there, too, because, of course, he made them laugh. Hiding their paintbrushes and fashioning mustaches on their sculptures of cats delighted them no matter what language they spoke.

And although he hadn't intended to, on Sunday Rudy found himself doing what Aunt Gussie had "suggested" and drawing caricatures of Jesus. The lesson was about the Lord turning over the moneychangers' tables in the temple. In Rudy's drawing, Jesus ended up looking a lot like Judge Caduff, and the moneychangers all resembled Al Capone and his men, but Rudy decided he liked it that way.

He looked over his drawings that afternoon after Sunday dinner, lying on his stomach on his bed. His favorite, Rudy decided, was his redoing of Jesus with the children on His lap. There was only one kid on His lap this time, and that was Rudy himself. He'd tried to make it funny—tried making bunny ears with his fingers behind Jesus' head—but it hadn't worked. It just looked like two fellas having a serious conversation.

Wonder what they're talking about? Rudy thought. And then

he snickered. *I should know. I drew it!* He was mulling over the possibilities when the door was flung open and Little Al burst in. Rudy didn't have time to stuff the drawing under the pillow before Little Al had joined him and was looking it over. The little guy could sure move fast.

"I know that's you," he said, pointing to the drawing of Rudy. "But who's this guy? He looks tough."

"He is," Rudy said, before he even thought about it, "tough as Al Capone—only He never breaks the law."

He was sure Little Al was going to start yelling about Rudy lecturing him just like everybody else. Little Al's mouth was getting tighter by the second, but he was still studying the drawing.

"Let me ask you somethin', Rudolpho," he said.

"Sure."

"You really think what the Boss is doin' is wrong? I'm not talkin' about whether it's illegal. What I wanna know is this: Is it really wrong to do whatever you have to do to protect your family and your territory? I mean, you say this guy is decent." He tapped the sketch of Jesus. "Would He say it was wrong?"

"Yeah," Rudy said.

"What would He do if somebody insulted His wife?"

"I don't think He's married."

"Or came in where He was doin' business and tried to take over?"

"I don't know," Rudy said. His stomach was churning like wash water.

"Huh," Little Al said. He pondered it for only a second longer, and then he scrambled off the bed. "Come on," he said. "We're goin' to the lake. Aunt Gussie says that's the only place to getta breath of cool air today."

It took Rudy the whole ride to Lake Michigan on their bikes to stop feeling stupid because he hadn't been able to answer Little

Al's questions. But by the time they parked and locked up their bikes at the pier and headed down onto the sand, Rudy realized that at least Little Al had asked. Maybe he was going to figure it out for himself and give up his dream of being like Al Capone forever.

It was a swell day—swimming in the icy Lake Michigan waters; picnicking on the sand from a basket Quintonia had stuffed full of fried chicken and biscuits and into which Aunt Gussie had tucked Baby Ruth bars for everybody; running all over the beach, luring seagulls with bread, and then scaring them to death when they landed.

"You'll play a trick on just about anybody, won't you?" Little Al said admiringly.

"I guess so," Rudy said. And then he suggested they build a sand castle.

It was a tired but happy group that headed back to Prairie Avenue around four o'clock when the air was finally giving up its quest to bake the city of Chicago. Hildy Helen started singing "I Wanna Be Loved by You," because it was a modern hit, of course, and Little Al and Rudy were mocking her in high-pitched voices as they turned the corner to their house. Rudy nearly ran right into the back of Al as the little Italian brought his bike to a squealing halt.

"What on earth are the police doing here?" Aunt Gussie said, braking behind Little Al.

There was indeed a long, rectangular police car at the curb, its fenders flaring out like angry nostrils in front. Rudy had never seen one close up, and he called to Little Al, "You think we could sit in it?"

"I ain't goin' nowhere near it!" Little Al said. "Miss Gustavia, thanks for everything, but I gotta be gettin' home. Mind if I borrow this bike?"

"I certainly do mind," Aunt Gussie said, dismounting hers

and handing it to Sol, who had approached from the gate. "Come along inside and have something to drink. You'll dehydrate after this hot ride."

"I don't care if I turn into a frog!" Little Al said. "If it's all the same to you, I don't feel like meetin' up with any coppers today."

"It isn't all the same to me, thank you. The police are our friends. I'm sure they're just here doing business with James."

Rudy saw Little Al's face go white as he followed Aunt Gussie reluctantly toward the house. He knew his own face was getting pale, and he didn't blame Little Al for glancing over his shoulder for an escape route. Aunt Gussie and Sol had all the exits blocked.

Dad met them in the front hall, and Rudy knew the minute he saw his father's face that something was wrong. Jim Hutchinson's nose was pinched, and his mouth was in a thin, straight line.

"To what do we owe the honor?" Aunt Gussie said.

Dad shook his head. "It's not an honor, I'm afraid."

Rudy poked Hildy Helen in the side, "All right, Hildy, what did you do this time? They finally caught you."

"And it isn't a joke, either," Dad said.

Mr. Hutchinson's eyes then darted around a little, as if he didn't want them to stop where they had to. Rudy caught his breath. Finally, Dad looked at Little Al. "They're here for you," he said.

Like an unexpected bolt of lighting, Little Al seemed to rise right up out of the floor and head for the door. But Sol was standing there, his arms folded, and in spite of his age, he looked like a wall Little Al could never get past. For the first time, as Little Al turned back to Dad, Rudy saw fear in his little friend's eyes.

"They sent the police because of some stolen apple?" Hildy Helen said.

Dad shook his head. "No, it's worse than that. Al, they're here about the Baby Joe Esposito shooting. They seem to think you were involved in that."

Rudy thought he was going to consume himself in fear, but Little Al let out a tight laugh. "Me?" he said. "Mr. Hutchie, I'm only small time! What are they thinking?"

"We're thinkin' somebody sang for us," said a voice from the library doorway.

It came from a broad-shouldered man in a brown policeman's frock coat. He hooked his thumbs in the black belt around his waist and didn't give even a hint of a smile as he lowered his eyes to Little Al.

"Somebody sang?" Hildy Helen said. "I don't get it."

"Means somebody squealed on your friend, young lady," the policeman said.

"Who?" Al cried. "Who ratted on me?"

He cast his eyes around desperately, and Hildy Helen took a step backward. "It wasn't Rudy or me, Al!" she said. "We'd never tell anything you told us."

Rudy wanted to crawl into the mummy case. He didn't get a chance to before Dad's face took on a we'll-talk-about-this-later expression.

"You know some fellas by the name of Daniel Torrio and Vincent Genna?" said the policeman.

"Sure," Little Al said. "They're friends of mine. Or they *were*."

Rudy felt stung for him. It would be like Hildy Helen telling on *him*.

"They came forward with some information that leads us to believe you were involved in Baby Joe's shooting. I'm going to take you down the station, ask you a few questions."

"Then can he come right back?" Hildy Helen said.

"Depends on the answers, little lady," said the policeman. He turned to Little Al. "I think you'll come along quiet-like. No need to put cuffs on you, eh?"

"I would."

It was the first time Aunt Gussie had spoken since they'd gathered in the hall. Her eyes were glinting fire, and Rudy was sure he'd never seen her face so stiff.

"Auntie, I don't think—" Dad started to say.

But she put up her hand to stop him. "I mean it, James," she said. "I've spent more time with the boy than you have. I know what kinds of little tricks he's capable of. If this officer ever intends to get him to the station, he's going to have to put him in handcuffs *and* leg irons, as far as I'm concerned."

She took in a long, deep, angry breath through her nose. Rudy felt a little angry himself.

"That's not true!" he said. "Little Al's not a criminal!"

"He almost had me convinced of that, too, Rudolph," Aunt Gussie said. "But as you see, he had us both fooled, and your father as well."

"I think I can speak for myself."

All eyes went to Jim Hutchinson, who was looking hard at his aunt. He pushed his glasses up his nose abruptly. "I'm not convinced of Al's involvement in this," Dad said. "I am the boy's attorney. I'm going to see to it that he is treated fairly."

"Just as he's treated us?" Aunt Gussie said.

"He's a boy!"

"Boy or not," the policeman said, "he's got to come with me. You can follow us to the station if you want, Mr. Hutchinson."

"Sol," said Dad, "will you drive me?"

Sol looked at Aunt Gussie, who merely sniffed, turned on the heel of her sensible pump, and stomped off into the parlor.

It was over in a matter of seconds. The officer ushered Little Al out the door and Dad followed with Sol, instructing him to drive as fast as he dared so they didn't miss a moment of being with Little Al while he was being questioned. When the door closed behind them, the house was deadly silent until Hildy Helen stamped her foot, nearly jiggling the ceremonial drum off its stand.

"They can't just take him like that!" she cried. Her fists balled up, and her face started on its way toward purple.

"I don't think throwing a tantrum is going to do any good," Rudy said.

"What will then?" Hildy Helen said. "What, Rudy?"

But Rudy shook his head slowly. "I don't know," he said.

They hoped Dad would know, and they waited for him on the steps in front of the door. Aunt Gussie never reappeared, and from the way Picasso was muttering nervously to himself in his cage, even he could sense the frosty feeling she had cast over the house.

When their father finally came back long after nine o'clock that night, Rudy was on him.

"Where's Little Al?" he said.

"Still at the station."

"Why?"

"They're putting him under arrest."

"No!" Hildy Helen cried. "They can't do that! He's only 10 years old!"

"You can get him off, can't you, Dad?" Rudy said.

Their father took off his hat and wearily ran a hand across his wavy, dark hair. It was lying heavily on his head, as if he'd been sweating for hours.

"I don't think so," he said. "There is more than just Danny and Vincie's statements. There's hard evidence that Little Al was part of the setup to get Joe Esposito to the train station that day."

He looked at them over the top of his rimless glasses. "And I think you know that."

Hildy Helen crossed her arms and refused to look at him. But Rudy couldn't seem to take his eyes away from his father's face.

"He did tell us he was in on it," he said. "We shoulda told you."

"Rudy!" Hildy Helen said.

"He's right," Dad said. "If I had known about this I might have been able to do something to avoid this whole situation. As it is, well, at least I know the truth. If I can get Little Al to own up to it, things will go better for him."

"Don't tell him we ratted on him," Hildy Helen said, glaring at Rudy.

"You didn't 'rat,'" Dad said. "You can't help your friend by going along with him."

"How *do* we help him, then?" Rudy said miserably.

"I'm not sure you can, but I think *I* can." Dad put an arm on each of their shoulders and led them toward the library. "You see," he said, "Little Al is just the kind of kid—"

"Just the kind of kid!" Picasso squawked out. "Just the kind of kid we've been looking for!"

Hildy Helen wrenched herself away. "It *was* Little Al you were talking about!"

Dad looked a little confused. "Little Al is just the kind of kid Judge Caduff and I have been waiting for, yes."

"For what?" Hildy Helen said.

Rudy wished she'd shut up. He didn't want to know.

"He's the perfect one to test our case—" Dad began.

Rudy didn't wait to hear the rest. He hurled himself around and headed for the stairs. Aunt Gussie cut him off at the pass.

"Rudy, wait!" Dad said.

"No!" Rudy cried. "If you're going to use Little Al for some kind of experiment, I don't want to hear about it! He's a real friend!"

"I beg your pardon, Rudolph," Aunt Gussie said, "But Alonzo Delgado is not our friend. He's merely a boy we tried to help, and we failed." She turned to Dad. "James, I think it is foolish for you to involve yourself in this any further. Let the boy go to prison and serve his time."

"For what, Auntie?" Dad said quietly. "For being used by a bunch of hoods with no conscience? Or for making you look like a fool because you cared?"

Aunt Gussie didn't answer but took herself stiffly into the library and slammed the door behind her, muttering something about taking stock of her artifacts to see if anything were missing. Rudy wouldn't look at his father.

"I think you've misunderstood me, Rudy," Dad said. "I want to help Little Al," Dad said. "I don't want to see him go to prison."

"You don't really care about him," Rudy said. "You care about your test case."

"I care about a human being," Dad said. His voice was hard and firm, and it made Rudy look up. "This isn't a chance for me to make a name for myself or prove something," Dad said. "I couldn't care less about my image. A person should never let that cover his true self."

Rudy waited.

"I've become very fond of Little Al," Dad said. "I want to see him make it. What Judge Caduff and I have been working on may be his only hope. Do you see?"

"No," Rudy said.

Dad sighed. "I hope you will," he said.

After that, Rudy and Hildy Helen didn't see their father for days. He buried himself in his work. And Little Al sat in jail waiting for his trial. Hildy Helen tried to cheer Rudy up. She couldn't, of course, not with a joke or an idea for a trick or any of the other things that usually worked. Finally, she wisely left him alone.

As for Aunt Gussie, Rudy refused to speak to her. He locked himself in his room every day when it was time to go to Hull House. After a while she stopped trying to roust him out and left him at home, where he drew pictures and sat in the window and sulked.

About the third day, when she and Hildy Helen returned to the house, Aunt Gussie didn't knock on his door but let herself in with a key and marched right over to his bed. He didn't even hide the rude drawing he'd made of her, walking like an angry goose checking for stolen articles. He wanted her to see what he thought of her.

Her eyes darted to it, and then to Rudy's face.

"Come along, Rudolph," she said. "We're going out."

"No," Rudy said.

"That really wasn't a question requiring an answer," she said. "It was an order."

"You're gonna have to drag me, then," Rudy said.

"Very well." She made a grab for his shoulder, and Rudy came off the bed. The only thing worse than talking to her would be having her touch him.

"All right! All right!" Rudy said.

He rode in sullen silence in the backseat of the Pierce Arrow, only staring out the window so he wouldn't have to look at Aunt Gussie. He really didn't see anything until Sol pulled the car up to the front of a massive building with impressive looking columns and a pair of majestic bronze lions that guarded the steps.

"It's the Art Institute of Chicago," Aunt Gussie said. "Inside. Let's go."

Rudy was careful to stay several feet behind Aunt Gussie and only grunted at her when she asked questions.

"There is much to see," she said, leading him up a graceful staircase.

I'm not going to see anything, Rudy told himself stubbornly. *She can drag me around all she wants, but I don't have to look at anything!*

And at first he didn't. He kept his eyes glued to the floor and continued grunting and growling as Aunt Gussie exclaimed in a whisper over Van Gogh and Monet and a bunch of other strange-sounding names he didn't care about. He didn't look up until Aunt Gussie said suddenly, "Ah! Picasso!"

"Where?" Rudy said. "Here?"

He looked around for the parrot and found himself standing in front of a zany looking painting of what appeared to be three comical men playing disjointed clarinets and guitars and a crazy piano. The colors danced and made Rudy want to snicker.

"*Three Musicians*," Aunt Gussie said. "One of my favorites of Picasso's work."

Rudy decided it wouldn't hurt to ask maybe one question. "Who's Picasso?"

"An artist," Aunt Gussie said. "I took such a liking to him I named my parrot after him."

"You know him?" Rudy said.

"Only through his work. There's more over here."

Rudy followed her to another wall where an oil painting showed a woman all made of rectangles and cubes and squares playing a round-looking guitar.

"*Girl with Mandolin*," Aunt Gussie said.

Rudy cocked his head and looked at it for a long time. "It's almost real, but it isn't," he said finally.

"Precisely. It is Picasso's idea of what is real. Has it never occurred to you that people see things differently? That you and I, for instance, see things differently from each other?"

"And how!" Rudy said. "Nobody thinks more different than you and me!"

She didn't answer but wandered on. Rudy spent a few more minutes looking at the girl with the mandolin and then followed Aunt Gussie into the next room. After that, a week could have gone by and Rudy would never have known it—not while he was gazing at Picasso's big-nosed *Self-Portrait*; or being given the willies by *Celestina*, who had a closed transparent eyelid; or staring at *Woman in an Armchair* long enough to see the disjointed woman as a whole without really having to find each separate part with his eyes. But it was when he went around the corner and saw *Mother and Child* that he did more than look. He *felt*—from somewhere deep down in his stomach.

The mother in the picture was big and solid looking, almost like a man, and on her lap was a chubby baby, who was reaching his arms up to touch her face while playing with his foot. They both seemed so content, as if the two of them could be at home anywhere, as long as they were together. As it was, there was very little background at all. They were in the middle of nothing and just—just being. It wasn't until Aunt Gussie put her hand on his shoulder that Rudy realized he was having trouble not crying.

"It moves you," she said.

"It's moving my stomach," Rudy said.

"That must be where you feel your passion," Aunt Gussie said.

Rudy shook his head and tried to move on, but Aunt Gussie held firmly to his shoulder.

"What is it that rumbles your stomach, Rudolph?" she said. "I'd like to hear."

"I don't know," he said.

"Does it make you think of your own mother you never knew?"

Rudy waited for his stomach to tell him the answer. There was nothing. "No," he said. "It's not my mother. It's just—nah, I'm bein' a sissy."

"Bigger men than you are sissies then," she said. "Go on."

"It makes me think of Little Al," he blurted out. "And you don't care about Little Al, so I don't want to talk about it."

"I do," she said. Her voice was so low, Rudy barely heard it. It kept him rooted to the floor.

"He didn't ever have that, I know it," Rudy said, pointing to the painting. "He thought he belonged to the Italian family, but they squealed on him. They just got jealous and turned on him."

"Go on."

"He'll never be happy like that kid in the painting. That's what I was thinkin'," Rudy said. "And if he goes to prison—"

He couldn't finish because he didn't know what to say.

"He'll lose his innocence," Aunt Gussie said.

Rudy wasn't sure what that meant, but he nodded. They stood in front of the painting for a while longer, and Rudy's stomach started to rear up again. He turned quickly to Aunt Gussie.

"That painting, Aunt Gussie," he said. "It's talking to me. Do you think I'm crazy?"

"Ah, Rudolph," she said.

And then something surprising happened. Slowly, surely, Aunt Gussie's stern mouth softened and her eyes began to twinkle. It took a second for Rudy to realize they were filled with tears.

"No more violin lessons for you, Rudolph," she said. "And no more opera or ballet. Movies yes, and I think some art classes are in order for you. Painting. Sculpting."

"Why?" Rudy said.

"Because art is your passion. You have an understanding at 10 years old some people never have all their lives. It shows who you are."

Rudy forced a laugh over the gurgling in his middle. "How do you know?" he said.

"Because," she said, "this is the first conversation we have ever had in which you didn't try to cover your feelings with jokes." She smiled down at him. "That, Rudy, is how I know who you are."

✢ ✢ ✢

Chapter Eighteen

*T*he next afternoon when Aunt Gussie had left to accompany Hildy Helen to her tennis lesson, Rudy found himself alone in the house and restless. He couldn't even settle down to do a drawing, even though back in his mind he wanted to try some of the things he'd seen in Picasso's paintings.

He tried to teach Picasso the parrot to say, "I like an old doll like you," in a Little Al voice, but the bird just blinked at him and ruffled a few feathers.

Rudy also tried playing a phone prank. When a woman answered a number he chose at random, Rudy said, "Madam, is your vacuum cleaner running?" When she answered, "Yes, it is," he said, "Then you'd better go catch it!" and hung up.

Why wasn't that as much fun as I always thought it would be? he wondered as he put the phone back on the desk.

It didn't take him long to figure out the answer. It was because it didn't help Little Al. That was all he really wanted to do, and all the tricks he could think of wouldn't get his friend out of jail. For the first time ever, he thought, *It won't do any good to play a prank.*

It was almost like Aunt Gussie saying, "Your uniqueness isn't worth much unless it's used for good."

Rudy tried to shake that off. Even after their trip to the art institute, Rudy still wasn't sure he could ever trust Aunt Gussie again.

But the thought wouldn't leave him alone, even as he fed Picasso some chunks of banana and fiddled with the ceremonial drum in the hallway and crawled into the mummy case and listlessly out again. *Use what you do for good. Just like Jesus.*

Finally, Rudy sat down on the bottom step of the staircase and put his face in his hands. If there was ever a time for an emergency prayer, it was now. *God*, he prayed, *would You please help me do something to help Little Al? He shouldn't go to prison, Lord. He's not as bad as everybody thinks. He was getting real close to quitting his bad life, I know he was. Please, help. I wouldn't ask, except this is an emergency. Amen, Rudy.*

It was a while before he got up from the step. He sat staring at the music room door and imagining Little Al in there having a lesson with Leo. That would never happen again. He'd never have a chance for a decent life again. There had to be something Rudy could do.

At first there were wild thoughts of breaking into the jail and rescuing Little Al from behind bars. But if there were a way to get out, Little Al himself would have found it by now. He was much better at these things than Rudy.

All I know how to do is play tricks to make people scream. I don't want to make Little Al scream—although I'd sure like to make Danny and Vincie squall their heads off for what they did to him.

And there it was: the one thing Rudy could do with his "uniqueness" that might be good. He could at least get revenge for Little Al on the boys who had done him wrong.

It was the first idea he'd been able to hang on to, and he did, with every ounce of his imagination. He knew what to do; the question now was how?

He glanced around the front hall, his eyes catching on the clock. Aunt Gussie and Hildy Helen would be home any minute. He'd have to use what he could get his hands on fast. One more long look around the library and Rudy had the beginnings of a plan.

He took the steps two at a time and plunged into the linen closet, coming out with two neatly ironed pillowcases. Back downstairs, he stuffed the ceremonial drum into one pillowcase, and looked longingly at the mummy case. Too bad it was so big; it was guaranteed to scare the pants off those Italians. But maybe the shell mask would be almost as good. He grabbed that and put it in his makeshift sack with the drum. Then he headed for the library.

This next step was going to be the hardest, especially if Quintonia were within earshot. One good squawk out of Picasso and she'd be there with her cast-iron skillet, ready to deliver a whammy to anyone who was "messin' with Miss Gustavia's birdie." His head already ringing at the thought, Rudy tiptoed gently into the room and approached Picasso's cage.

"Hey, fella," he whispered.

Picasso jerked a wing.

"I got somethin' for ya," Rudy said.

"Baby Ruth," Picasso said. His voice was low like Rudy's. Rudy broke into a grin.

"If that's what you want," Rudy said. "Wait right here."

Picasso blinked and watched him as Rudy went quickly to Aunt Gussie's desk, reached into the bottom left-hand drawer, and fished out a candy bar. He paused a second, then grabbed another one and crammed it into his pocket.

He unwrapped the first Baby Ruth and stuck it down in the bottom of the empty pillowcase. Then he unlatched the cage and held the case open in front of it.

"Come and get it, Picasso," he whispered. "Got your treat right here in the bag."

"Baby Ruth," Picasso said. His voice was low and almost pitiful as he put one trusting claw in front of the other and emerged from the cage. He hesitated for a moment at the opening to the pillowcase and blinked. "Baby Ruth?" he said.

Rudy swallowed hard. "I wouldn't do it if it weren't for Little Al," Rudy said to the bird. "We have to help him. Go on in. It's down at the bottom."

He edged the case's opening toward Picasso. The parrot went headfirst into the pillowcase. Rudy closed it behind him and held on tight.

"Baby Ruth!" Picasso said with delight.

Rudy had no idea how long it would take a parrot to devour a sticky candy bar, but he knew he had to be out of the house and down the road before he finished it and started squawking. The kind of fuss he was going to put up would bring a shrunken head back to life.

Grateful for that thought, Rudy hurried through the front hallway with his two sacks, grabbed the shrunken head and dumped it in with the ceremonial drum and the mask, and made for the front door. The instant he got there, he heard the Pierce Arrow pull into the driveway.

Rudy dashed to the door that led out into the courtyard. He'd have to wait out there until Aunt Gussie and Hildy Helen were safely inside the house, and then he'd wriggle through the "tunnel" in the stone wall and take the back way toward the West Side. It was going to be chancy with Picasso in the sack, but it was a risk he had to take. It was, after all, for Little Al.

God, are You there? he remembered to pray, even though it wasn't an emergency—yet.

As soon as he heard the front door close, Rudy made a beeline for the tunnel. Inside the sack, Picasso was beginning to mutter.

"Shhhh!" Rudy hissed as he fell to his belly and pushed both sacks into the tunnel in front of him. With a deep breath, he thrust his head inside the tunnel and started to worm his way through. One more wriggle and all of him would be inside, and then he was safe.

But something grabbed on to his ankle and froze him. Picasso's muttering grew louder.

"Rudy Hutchinson, what is going on?" whispered a voice from the mouth of the tunnel.

"Let go!" Rudy hissed back at Hildy Helen. "I hafta get out of here!"

"Not without me, you're not!"

"Hilde-garde!" a dry voice called out from inside the house. "Have you seen Rudolph?"

"Move!" Hildy Helen said as loud as she dared. "I'm comin' in!"

Rudy squirmed ahead with his elbows, still pushing his sacks in front of him. By now, Picasso was working himself into a mumbling frenzy.

"Want another candy bar?" Rudy whispered to him as he continued to scoot forward. "Want another Baby Ruth?"

"Baby Ruth," Picasso cried.

Rudy made the final heave out onto the sunny sidewalk and scrambled to his feet.

Hildy Helen was right behind him, her cheeks blotchy red and eyes wide.

"What are we doing?" she said.

There was no point in telling her she couldn't come. She was already several steps ahead of him as they tore up Prairie Avenue, and she was being careful to keep them behind trees and in the shadows. The caper was half hers already.

"We're getting revenge," Rudy told her, "on those lousy squealers."

"What's in the bags?" she said.

Rudy told her, and he explained what he was going to do. "Better let me carry one," she said.

He gladly turned Picasso over to her. The bird was starting to squawk again.

By then they were headed down in back of Prairie and would soon be behind Aunt Gussie's house. Hildy Helen stopped Rudy, and they both panted and smeared the Chicago sweat from their faces.

"The garage is right here," she said. "Wouldn't it be faster if we took the bikes?"

"We won't be able to take fire escapes and jump off walls with bikes."

"So, we get to Little Italy, then we stash the bikes someplace, do what we have to do, and then go back for them."

Rudy couldn't help grinning. They made such a good team. The thought that Little Al made them an even better one sobered him up.

"The only problem is Sol," Hildy Helen was saying. "If he's in the garage—"

"Baby Ruth!" Picasso cried.

"Shh!" said Hildy.

But Rudy poked her and pointed to the bag, and Hildy Helen grinned with him.

Moments later as they peered cautiously through the dusty garage window and saw Sol in his undershirt and his green uniform pants dozing on a chair in the corner, Rudy nodded to Hildy Helen. She opened the pillowcase where Picasso was just finishing his second Baby Ruth of the day and whispered—"Fire! Fire in the kitchen! That blasted toaster!"

Picasso proved himself to be a trusty member of the team, too. Right on cue, he cried out, "Fire! Fire in the kitchen! Blasted toaster! Blasted toaster!"

Rudy watched through the circle he cleared on the window dust as Sol jerked from the chair, sending it toppling to the floor. Eyes still wild with sleep, the old chauffeur made for the garage door, while Picasso continued to egg him on with, "Fire! Fire in the kitchen! Toaster! Toaster!"

The instant Sol disappeared, Hildy Helen had Rudy by the arm, and together they stormed the garage. The bicycles were waiting conveniently near the door, and they hopped on, each with a bulging pillowcase in hand, and made their hasty exit.

Hildy Helen led the way until they reached Taylor Street in Little Italy, and then she slowed down so Rudy could get past her.

"We're going to Uncle Anthony's store," Rudy said over his shoulder. "The bikes'll be safe out in back."

Rudy led his sister through a maze of alleys that were arched with clotheslines and smelled of garlic. He thought a few times that he was lost, but something familiar would always pop up in front of him and he rode on. Finally, they pulled up behind Uncle Anthony's grocery and dismounted. Rudy directed Hildy Helen to lean the bikes on the wall.

"They do blend in with all the other junk," she said. "Sol would have a fit if he saw this mess."

Sol, Rudy figured, was having a fit about something entirely different about now. That made him want to hurry even more.

"Can you keep Picasso quiet?" Rudy said as he took off with Hildy down the alley.

"If I keep feeding him. Do you have any more Baby Ruths?"

Rudy shook his head, but he stopped briefly at a garbage can and pulled out a half-eaten apple.

Two things happened as they rounded the end of the block and peeked out into Taylor Street, where the front of the grocery was. Both of them stirred Rudy's stomach as if there were a stick in there.

One, a menacing rumbling came from the distant sky. Rudy

looked up and for the first time realized that the sunny summer afternoon was quickly growing dark with an awning of black clouds.

"Don't worry about rain, Rudy," Hildy Helen said. "It'll just cool us off."

But the other thing that caught Rudy's attention wasn't so easily dealt with. As he peered down the block, he made out two figures stationed in front of Uncle Anthony's grocery like a pair of sentries guarding an entrance. At first he didn't recognize them; he'd never seen them so stiff and tense and wary before. But as he blinked and looked again, there was no doubt about it. Danny and Vincie were only a hundred feet away.

"Get back!" Rudy hissed to Hildy Helen.

"Why?" she said as she followed orders for once.

"They're right there!"

"Well, that's good isn't it? Now we don't have to hunt them down."

Rudy scanned the busy street with his eyes. "I was hoping we'd meet up with them in a back alley. Our trick is going to be hard to pull off with people around."

Once again the sky rumbled, and Hildy Helen looked up. "They won't be around for long. As soon as those clouds break open, everybody will be running for cover."

"Yeah, but Danny and Vincie will just go inside the store."

"They can't if the front door's locked, though, can they?" Hildy Helen said.

"Who's gonna lock it?"

Hildy Helen smiled slyly. "Get ready. I'll go in through the back door and lock the front. When they can't get in, they'll have to turn around, and there you'll be with that." She pointed to Rudy's bag, and before he could protest, she was gone, Picasso swinging after her in his own sack.

"Don't forget, you have to come right back. I need him," Rudy hissed to her.

It wasn't a perfect plan, but it was the best they had. Rudy watched Hildy disappear back into the alley, and then he got busy with the pillowcase.

He was ready for what seemed like hours before a fork of lightning cut in close to Taylor Street and a jarring clap of thunder followed it. Finally, the first heavy drops of rain hit the pavement, and Rudy craned his neck to see down the block.

"Sissies," he whispered to himself. The very instant Vincie felt a raindrop hit the back of his neck, he was hurling himself into the entryway. The entrance was indented and Rudy couldn't see the door, but a moment later both Danny and Vincie were back on the sidewalk, pulling up their collars and squinting through the torrent that was starting to pelt them. Hildy Helen had completed her mission.

Now it was time for Rudy's. While Danny and Vincie shouted at each other about whose fault it was that they were stuck out in a blinding thunderstorm, Rudy ducked into the entrance of a shoe repair shop two doors from the grocery and hoped the boys would decide to head this way. The mask was in place on his face. The drum was securely fastened to the waistband of his knickers. The shrunken head was swinging by its hair behind his back.

It was hard to hear anything over the rain and the thunder, but Rudy made out the sound of sloshing footsteps coming his way. With one last emergency prayer, he dove out onto the sidewalk. The two boys stopped and stared.

Rudy gave the drum a couple of ominous beats before he leaned forward and shouted, "Are you the ones?"

"Ones what?" Vincie said. His big lips were trembling.

Danny gave him an elbow jab. "Who're you?" he said to Rudy.

"I come on behalf of Alonzo Delgado!" Rudy shrieked, shaking the mask. "Are you the ones who delivered his soul to the police?"

"We didn't deliver no soul!" Vincie cried. "We just told them what he done. He deserved it!"

"Would you shut up!" Danny said. He squinted his eyes at Rudy. "Come on—who are you?"

Rudy threw back his head and cackled loudly through the mask. When he brought his face back up, he also pulled the shrunken head from behind his back. Two pairs of eyes doubled in size. "Here's what's left of your friend!" Rudy cried. "And he has something to say to you!"

Then Rudy held his breath. Nothing happened. Where was Hildy Helen? Vincie, he was sure, would stand there all day, too frozen with fear to even wet his trousers. But Danny was already studying the head. Rudy made it swing.

"So what's this message?" Danny said.

Rudy held the head up high in the air and closed his eyes. *Come on, Hildy Helen*, he thought. *Get here with Picasso!*

The sky suddenly seemed to open up and explode in one giant crash of thunder. When Danny jumped, Rudy swung the head close to his face and shouted, "There's your message of doom!"

Vincie was the first to scream, but Danny turned and was off down the sidewalk. Rudy was grinning behind his mask when a voice behind him hissed, "After them!"

Hildy Helen gave Rudy a shove, and they bolted in the wake of the terrified Italians. Hildy Helen pulled out ahead of Rudy and fumbled with the pillowcase. Above the din of the storm, Rudy could hear Picasso crying, "Sold my soul! Sold my soul! You'll pay! You'll pay!"

Both boys stiffened and stopped. Rudy did, too, and waited for Hildy Helen to do as they'd planned and duck into a store entrance. But she couldn't seem to resist just one more warning from Picasso.

"You'll pay! Awk! You'll pay!"

Hildy was just in the act of diving under the awning of a clock

shop when Danny whirled around. He was after Hildy Helen before she could get one foot into the entryway. Lip still hanging
down to his chin, Vincie followed.

Enough screaming burst from the storefront to shrink a
whole tribe of heads. Some of it Rudy recognized as Picasso's
squawking. The rest was coming from Hildy.

That was what peeled his feet from the sidewalk and got him
to the entrance. By now his mask was cockeyed and he could
barely see through the holes. He yanked it off and tossed it into
a puddle—and stared at the scene in front of him.

Hildy Helen was backed up against the door, both arms held
up above her head and plastered against the glass by Vincie's
angry hands. Danny had his face an inch from Hildy's, teeth
clenched, and he was talking to her in a low, sinister tone.

"You think makin' fools of us is gonna change anything?"
Each word sounded as if Danny were spitting it. "We'll do worse
than that to you, ya little Bug-Eyed Betty! We'll show ya how to
get revenge!"

What he had in mind, Rudy never knew. Before Danny could
make his next move, Rudy flung himself at the boy's back and
sunk his teeth into the back of his neck. Danny gave a yelp and
threw his arms behind him, throwing Rudy, behind-first, onto the
sidewalk. The tall Italian then stood over him, rain pouring from
his hair, fists clenched, and planted his foot squarely in Rudy's
middle—so hard his stomach couldn't even begin to churn. It
was over. There was no way to escape the onslaught of those ready
fists.

Except that, from the entrance, another cry was heard—this
time from an angry bird who had finally escaped from a certain
pillowcase. He sent up such a screech that Danny twisted his head
to look. As he did, Picasso flapped wildly away from Hildy Helen
and straight into Danny's face.

His foot came off Rudy, who scrambled to his feet and started for Vincie. But the big-lipped boy was already cowering in the corner, his hands covering his face, whimpering, "Don't let it get me! Don't let it get me!"

When Rudy turned, Picasso had finished pecking at Danny's forehead and was flying in fits and starts around the store entrance way. Danny stood bent at the waist, holding his head and moaning.

"Get him!" Hildy Helen hissed at Rudy. "Get him now!"

She pointed furiously at the heavy drum Rudy held around his waist. Snatching it up in both hands, Rudy held it over Danny's head.

This is for stealing my bike—and for turning in Little Al—and for threatening my sister! his thoughts screamed. *Now you are gonna find out what revenge really is!*

Rudy pulled the drum back. But even as he flung it forward, he knew something was wrong. He knew he couldn't do it. The only thing he didn't know was why.

He let the drum drop loose on its tether and reached for Hildy Helen's wrist. "Come on!" he said, and dragged her out into the downpour.

"You didn't hit him!" Hildy Helen shrieked at him as they tore down the sidewalk. "You chickened out!"

Rudy just glanced over his shoulder. Nobody was following yet. He knew all they needed was two minutes to get themselves together and give some kind of signal and the street would be swarming with Dannies and Vincies, rain or no rain.

"Why didn't you hit him?" Hildy Helen continued to wail. "You could have hit both of them! Picasso did all that for nothing!"

Rudy came to a halt that sent a wave from a puddle up over their shoes. "Picasso!" he cried. "Did you get him?"

Hildy's face went to stone. "No," she said. "I thought he was with you."

Rudy ripped the drum from his waistband and thrust it at her so it wouldn't bang against his legs, and then he took off, back toward the store entry.

"Rudy, no!" Hildy Helen screamed after him.

He kept on, rain hammering his face like bullets, until he slammed head on into the chest of tall Danny Torrio.

Danny gripped both of Rudy's shoulders and brought him straight up like an exclamation point. When Danny jolted him close to his face, Rudy could see the claw marks on his cheek and a bloody spot on his nose where a chunk had been taken out.

"Where's the bird?" Rudy shouted at him.

"I don't know nothin' about no bird! I just want you to know one thing, so you listen good."

"No! Not until you give Picasso back!"

Vincie joined them then, rain pouring from his lower lip as if it were a gutter. "We don't know no Picasso. Is he from another gang?"

"He's a bird!" Rudy cried.

Danny gave him a shake that rattled his teeth. "Would ya shut up about the bird! Now you listen to me. Yeah, we squealed on Little Al, but he had it comin', y'see? And it's your fault—you and that little dame."

"Our fault?" Rudy said.

"Yeah, you took him out of the neighborhood. You made it easy for him to betray us, see? So we hadda even up the score."

With Rudy now maskless and imprisoned by Danny's hands, Vincie turned brave again. "Then you come down here, thinkin' *you* have a score to even up. Ha! Right Danny-boy?"

Danny nodded, but Rudy shook his head.

"No, that isn't right," Rudy said. "I mean—that's what we came for—but forget it. It doesn't do any good. It won't get Little Al out of jail."

Danny loosened his grip a little as he laughed. "You don't

think Al's gonna stay in jail, do ya? We Italians, we take care c
each other. He'll be out of the hoosegow in no time. Somebody'll
get him off. I'm surprised he ain't walking the streets already."

"Is that why you were standing out in front of his uncle's grocery store—so you could be the first ones to catch him?"

"Yeah!" Vincie said, his big mouth parting in a grin. "We still
gotta show him what happens to fellas that think they're better'n
everybody else."

"Shut up, Vincie," Danny said.

But it was too late. Rudy wrenched himself away from Danny's
loosened grip and took a step backward. He had to say one thing
to them, though, before he took off. "So Italians take care of their
own, huh? I'm sure glad I don't have somebody like you 'takin'
care' of me." And then before Danny could get out an answer he
spun around and ran, splashing, down the sidewalk. Hildy Helen
was waiting for him around the corner, eyes streaming as many
tears as there were raindrops.

"They didn't kill you!" she said when she saw him.

Rudy peered cautiously around the corner, but there was no
one following. The street was empty in the storm, except for one
car—a long, sleek Pierce Arrow that slowly cut through the
sheets of rain.

Rudy's stomach didn't churn. It just fell with a thud to the pit
of his soul.

"No, they didn't kill me," he said to Hildy Helen. "But somebody else is going to."

✠ ⬦ ✠

Chapter Nineteen

*R*udy peered around the corner once more and saw the Pierce Arrow stopped in front of Uncle Anthony's grocery store. He flattened himself against the wall and watched, Hildy Helen right beside him.

The back window opened, and a dry, crackly voice broke through the rain.

"Hildegarde!" it cried out. "Rudolph!"

"Wait, Rudy," Hildy Helen whispered. "When we don't answer, they'll drive on and then we can go back and look for Picasso."

She pulled him back around the corner, and they huddled on the back side of a cellar door, peeking over the top.

But no long, sleek car crawled by. Instead, Aunt Gussie's dry voice cracked wide open into the rain.

"Picasso!" she cried. "What in the name of all heaven are you doing *here?*"

Rudy slumped against the wall and let the downpour hit him in the face.

"Well, at least he isn't lost anymore," Hildy Helen said.

Rudy shrugged. "Let's get the bikes. We might as well go home."

"Maybe she'll be cooled off by the time we get there."

With a picture in his mind of Aunt Gussie working up a good head of steam, Rudy rounded the corner into the alley. Three doors down, he stopped abruptly, ankle deep in a muddy puddle, and stared.

"The bikes!" Hildy Helen cried. "What's happened to them?"

"Three guesses," Rudy said.

He didn't even have to go closer to see that the shiny, red bicycle and the shiny, blue one were now only twisted masses of metal. The wheels were hanging from a clothesline. The two seats had been fastened to the back of a skinny dog curled up next to the stoop. And the rest would be about as useful for getting them home as wishing for a magic carpet to appear. What Rudy wished for was the ground to open and swallow him up.

"Those miserable little—ugh!" Hildy Helen said.

Rudy looked at her balled up fists and her reddening face. "Don't bother," he said. "Let's just go find Aunt Gussie, or we're going to have to walk home."

When they got to the corner, Rudy wasn't surprised to see the Pierce Arrow parked there. The minute the twins headed toward the car, the back door opened and Aunt Gussie made room for them. As they slid inside, mud and all, Picasso muttered from his perch on his owner's shoulder, "Children in trouble. Children in trouble, Sol."

Sol looked in the mirror at the mud that was caking up his carefully polished leather seats.

"Yeah, we know," Hildy Helen mumbled.

Rudy couldn't say anything. He just waited for the torrent of words to come down on him from Aunt Gussie's mouth, harder than the rain.

But there was only silence as Sol drove the Pierce Arrow out of Little Italy. Hildy Helen couldn't stand it.

"We were just trying to help Little Al," she said. "We didn't know Picasso was going to get lost."

Picasso squawked, and Aunt Gussie soothed him with the palm of her hand.

"We shouldn'ta taken him in the first place," Rudy said. "We shouldn't of even come here at all. It didn't do any good."

Aunt Gussie looked at him quickly. "What didn't, Rudolph?" she said.

"Trying to get back at those boys that squealed on Little Al. It would only keep going on and on. And I just couldn't do it."

"What couldn't you do?" Aunt Gussie persisted.

"Hit that lousy Danny over the head with your drum," Hildy Helen said. Then to the window, she muttered, "*I* woulda done it."

"We shouldn'ta taken the drum, either," Rudy said.

"But I didn't lose that," Hildy Helen put in. "It's right here."

"Or the mask, or the shrunken head. They probably floated down the gutter by now."

Rudy stared down into his wet lap. It was the most horrible moment he'd ever had, and the ones ahead didn't promise to be much better. He couldn't think of another thing to say, funny or not.

"Rudy, look at me," Aunt Gussie said.

He only did because she hadn't called him "Rudolph." Her eyes were firm, but they weren't sharp.

"You had a chance to hit that boy over the head and get back at him for good, but you didn't. Do you know why?"

"I told you," Rudy said.

"I think there's another reason. Do you remember when I told you that you were more like Jesus than you knew?"

Rudy shrugged. "Jesus probably would've found a way to do *something*."

"But not the way you were going to do it. And even you stopped yourself. You took the risk to do what was good. You couldn't use your cleverness this time, because it wasn't for a good cause. That's the way Jesus was—He only did what He did if it was for God."

"It *was* for a good cause, though," Hildy Helen said. "We did it for Little Al." Her fists balled up again. "I know you don't think so, Aunt Gussie, but he's a good boy!"

"Forget it," Rudy said, looking back into his lap again. "There's no way I can save him. And it looks like not even Jesus will."

This time, Aunt Gussie was quiet.

To the twins' surprise, there was no punishment for their "borrowing" of Aunt Gussie's things or even for losing some of them, much less for leaving the property without permission and getting themselves mixed up with what Rudy heard Aunt Gussie refer to as "unsavory characters."

In fact, Aunt Gussie seemed to soften a little. She didn't reprimand either of them about manners at the supper table that night, and not a word was said about brushing teeth or being in bed on time.

Dad, too, used his lowest, kindest voice when he came home that night and took both of them into Rudy's room to talk. But what he had to say took any comfort out of their getting off, as Hildy Helen put it, "scot-free."

"Little Al's hearing is tomorrow afternoon," he told them. "And as hard as I've worked, I've not been able to get the charges dismissed. He has pled guilty. The hearing is to determine his sentence."

"What's going to happen to him?" Hildy Helen said.

"He'll go to prison unless I can convince the judge to make other arrangements, although I don't know what they would be. His own home obviously isn't a fit place."

"Judge Caduff?" Rudy said hopefully.

Dad shook his head. "Another judge—one who is on the crime

commission. He's all for throwing everyone who jaywalks into the Big House."

His voice had a hard edge, and Rudy shrank away from it. He didn't want to hear any more about Little Al going to prison. He groped for something funny to say, to make his father laugh, to make this all go away.

But there was nothing. Dad tucked them in and left Rudy in the dark. He fell asleep drawing a picture in his mind of Little Al, crouched in a corner of a cell in a darkness he might never get out of.

The next morning when Rudy got up, Hildy Helen and Aunt Gussie were already gone. When they came home at lunchtime, Rudy could only sit at the dining room table and stare at both of them with his mouth hanging open.

"Close your mouth, boy, before you drool on my tuna salad!" Quintonia said,

Then her eyes went to the pair in the doorway, and her own mouth fell open like an old leather satchel.

"Miss Gustavia, as I live and breathe!" she cried. "You done cut your hair!"

"*Bobbed* our hair," Hildy Helen said. She spun around in the dining room, thick, dark, chin-length hair bouncing against her cheeks. The sparkle was back in her eyes.

She stopped and glowered at Rudy, arms folded. "Do I look adorable? You haven't said."

But Rudy was too busy gaping at Aunt Gussie. She removed her hat to reveal her slate-gray hair clipped close and arranged in waves that rippled down the back of her head.

"I don't know why I didn't do this a long time ago, Quintonia," she said. "It's going to be so easy to take care of."

Rudy was still staring. She didn't look nearly so old and dried up now.

"I suppose you're wondering why your father and I changed

our minds about Hildy Helen's hair," Aunt Gussie said to him.

Hildy Helen poked Rudy in the ribs. "Wait 'til you getta load of this."

"Hildy Helen has shown me her passions," Aunt Gussie went on. "I have discovered who she is on the inside, and I think she has, too. Therefore, she can do whatever she wants with the outside." Aunt Gussie glanced at herself in the mirror. "And in discovering her, I've discovered a little more of myself as well."

Then she pointed her all-seeing eyes in Rudy's direction. "I have discovered your passion and your soul, too, Rudolph," she said. "But as yet I have not found a way to mark it. The good Lord, I suppose, will provide. We shall see."

When they arrived at the courthouse later that afternoon and Rudy was squirming nervously on the wooden bench Dad parked them on, Hildy Helen leaned over and whispered, "You know something, Rudy?"

He shook his head.

"I thought I'd feel so much more modern with my hair bobbed."

"Don't you?"

She shook her head. "I think I might have been modern already, and I didn't even know it."

Just then a door creaked open, and Little Al entered the courtroom, led by a poker-faced policeman. Rudy strained to get a good look at his friend. He wasn't hardened like Dad said he would be if he spent time in prison. Just then, he only looked white-faced and frightened around the mouth—not anything close to Al Capone.

Neither Little Al nor the policeman looked to the right or left as the officer nudged Al into a seat beside Dad. Rudy was glad to see his father put his arm around the boy's shoulders and give them a squeeze.

It's not going to do him much good, though, Rudy thought.

He tried to pray an emergency prayer, but even that seemed hopeless.

Just then a severe-looking judge in a black robe sailed into the front of the court from the opposite side. He climbed to his high bench and looked down at them as if everyone there were on trial. He had the largest nose Rudy had ever seen on a human being, but no drawing popped into his mind. He was only filled with terror for Little Al.

Aunt Gussie nudged Rudy on the other side, and he stood up with the rest of the people who had gathered to see Little Al's fate. Rudy sneaked a glance around. There was Judge Caduff, but Danny and Vincie were nowhere in sight. The only other Italian in the room as far as he knew was a man in the back row in a black fedora, which he had pulled low over his eyes. Rudy got a chill, and he stared at him with his head swiveled around, even after they sat down. The man remained tucked into the corner, his eyes invisible.

Aunt Gussie poked him again. "This is the first time I have seen your father in action," she said. "This is exciting."

Rudy wanted to poke her back hard. She still couldn't care less about Little Al. What was all that talk about image and what things looked like? What good was that if you didn't care about somebody?

Dad stood up and smoothed out his vest under his padded-shoulder suit. Rudy didn't remember having seen that suit, which fit quite well. Aunt Gussie had probably bought it for him for this "show."

But if his father was conscious of his smart-looking outfit, he didn't show it. Once he patted Little Al's shoulder and came out from behind the defense table, he seemed to have nothing on his mind but proving that Alonzo Delgado, in spite of his past mistakes, was a person with potential.

Dad told of the changes he had seen in Little Al since he'd

been coming to the house on Prairie Avenue and how eager he seemed to better himself. It would have been enough to convince Rudy even if he'd never met Al before. But then the lawyer for the prosecution—the district attorney—stood up in his pin-striped sack suit and began to tell of Little Al's numerous petty crimes. They all led up to his involvement in this murder, the district attorney said, and Al needed to be locked away before he did something even worse. There was a society to protect, after all. That made Aunt Gussie grunt.

Dad was on his feet again, and even from the back Rudy knew that his father's nose was tightly pinched.

"Alonzo Delgado only became a so-called threat to our society," he said, glaring at the other attorney, "when the only men he had to look up to were thieves and murderers. Which makes better sense to you, sir? To throw the boy in with no one *but* criminals and hope he learns not to be what they are? Or to keep him as far away from them as possible so he can see that there is a better way of life?"

The prosecutor smiled coldly. "And where do you propose we do this, Mr. Hutchinson? We have already seen that the boy's home is unfit."

The stern old judge was nodding fiercely. "He has a point, Counselor. And please do not torture the court with your idea of creating youth facilities. We have no such facility at present, so you would be wasting the court's time."

"I had no intention of doing anything of the kind, Your Honor," Dad said. "I am far more concerned about the fate of this promising young man than I am about my own ideas."

"Very commendable," said the judge. "And I assure you that if there were anyplace to send young Mr. Delgado where I was convinced he could be saved from a life of crime, I would send him there without batting an eye. But since it is my duty to up-hold justice and rid this city of crime—"

Beside Rudy there was a great rustling of starched cotton. Aunt Gussie was standing up.

"Your Honor, if I may," she said. Her dry voice crackled with authority. The judge raised his eyebrows, but he nodded to her.

"Mrs. Nitz," he said.

"Yes, Your Honor. May I be allowed to speak?"

Rudy hoped against hope that the judge would say no and tell her to sit back down. He could see his father's face turning pale. Little Al was purposely not looking at her at all.

"Does it pertain to the matter at hand?" said the judge.

Aunt Gussie shot up an eyebrow of her own. "Of course it does. I would like to offer a solution to this dilemma."

"In what way?"

"You can't cart him off to Hull House, if that's what you're thinking," the district attorney burst out.

"Does everyone in town know her?" Hildy Helen whispered.

"I don't want to take him to Hull House," Aunt Gussie said. "I want to take him to *my* house."

There was a startled silence, followed by a buzz the judge had to quiet with a bang of his gavel.

"Do you know what you are saying, Gussie?" he said, his face losing its sternness and crumpling into concern. "You are taking full responsibility for this boy, and for his actions."

"I know that. And I am willing to take that risk."

To Rudy's amazement, the judge actually chuckled. "You always were a risk-taker," he said.

"Only when it's for good," Aunt Gussie said. "And then it is no longer a risk—it's a duty. I would like to have custody of Alonzo."

There was a time when being in Aunt Gussie's "custody" would not have been something Rudy would have wished for anyone, especially Little Al. But Al himself obviously didn't think it was such a bad idea. He looked from Aunt Gussie to the judge and back again so many times Rudy's head began to spin. And there was something in Little Al's eyes he had never seen there before. It was a pencil-slim ray of hope.

"Very good, then," the judge said, looking down his huge nose. "I assign custody of one Alonzo Delgado to Mrs. Gustavia Nitz. Mr. Hutchinson, you will draw up the necessary papers?"

"Certainly, Your Honor," Dad said. He looked as if he could hardly keep himself from cheering out loud. Hildy Helen, too, could barely hold it in until they were outside the courtroom, waiting for Little Al to emerge a free man.

"This is—this is the bee's knees!" she cried. "It's the cat's pajamas! It's—"

"We get the idea, Hildegarde," Aunt Gussie said. "I will take that as a substitute for 'thank you.' "

"Thank you, Aunt Gussie," Rudy said. These were the first words he'd trusted himself to utter. Any more and he might have started crying.

"I appreciate that, Rudolph," Aunt Gussie said. "After all, I did this in part for you."

"Me?" Rudy said.

"I told you I wanted some way to mark the discovery of your passion."

"But I thought art was my passion."

"Art is an *expression* of your passion," Aunt Gussie said. "Your passion is for your fellow human beings. You try hard to cover it, son, but you care so deeply about other people, I think it hurts you inside sometimes."

He was glad she didn't ask him if he thought she were right. She only brushed his shoulder with her fingertips and turned to the courtroom door, which was opening behind them.

Little Al stepped out into the marble-floored lobby, looking small amid the pillars and the high ceilings. But there was nothing small about the way he walked right up to Aunt Gussie and put out his hand. She took it, and they shook.

"Thank you, madam," he said. "I appreciate what you've done for me, and I will do my best not to disappoint you."

"See that you don't," she said. "Or it's off to the Big House with you. I'm sticking my neck out for you, you know."

Little Al broke into a grin Rudy never thought he could have achieved with that tight little mouth. "You know somethin', Miss Gustavia?" he said. "I like an old doll like you."

There seemed to be nothing to do then but go out and celebrate. And Aunt Gussie said there was nowhere else *to* celebrate but The Cape Cod Room. If Rudy had thought Al grinned big before, he hadn't seen anything.

"The Cape Cod Room, Rudolpho!" he said when they were squeezed into the Pierce Arrow and headed for the Near West Side. "I always wanted to eat there. Never thought I would."

"Really?" said Aunt Gussie. "I thought you were going to grow up to be a mobster and eat there all the time."

Rudy held his breath. Couldn't the woman just leave well enough alone?

But it didn't seem to bother Little Al a bit. He gave one of his tight, knowing smiles. "I've had it with the mob," he said. "They'll fink on ya in a minute if it's their neck in the noose."

"Fink?" Hildy Helen said.

"New word I picked up in the hoosegow," Little Al said.

"Dreadful," Aunt Gussie said. "And don't think for a minute that you're going to teach it to Picasso."

"Nah, no more mob for me," Little Al went on. "I got more loyal friends—ones who'll try to do right by ya, no matter what." He looked at Rudy. His eyes said, *Thanks.*

Rudy nodded, and for a while there, everything was perfect.

When the group was happily digging into their desserts, the waiter came over and said in a low voice to Dad, "Sir, the gentleman in the booth would like to pick up the bill for your dinner."

Everyone at the table turned to stare at the booth. The curtain was closed, but as they watched, a man unfolded from within and stood looking back at them. Rudy and Hildy Helen gasped like one person.

It was the man in the black fedora, and Rudy knew he'd been right in the courtroom. He was sure that under the brim of that ever-present hat, the man's eyes had a cruel glint.

Rudy turned to his father and tugged at his sleeve. Dad lowered his head to listen.

"Don't take anything from them," Rudy whispered fiercely. "That guy was after Little Al—and us!"

Dad seemed to have a hard time not coming right up out of the chair. Instead, his nose pinched in. "He's one of Capone's. He was probably out to get Al to keep him from 'finking' to the police about who he was helping when Baby Joe was killed."

"Little Al never told?" Rudy whispered.

"No. I talked until I was blue in the face, and he wouldn't say a word." Dad stole a glance up at Little Al, who was still staring at the man in the fedora, a smug look on his little face. "We still have some ideas to clear up in Little Al's head."

Then he sat up and shook his head at the waiter. "Please tell the gentlemen that I appreciate their offer, but I can't accept it," he said, loudly enough for Mr. Black Fedora to hear him.

At last Rudy saw the familiar glint in the man's eyes. Black Fedora turned at once and dove back into the booth.

Once again things were perfect—laughter and spumoni and talk of things ahead.

"So where am I gonna sleep?" Little Al said.

"Can he share my room?" Rudy said.

"That would be asking for disaster," Aunt Gussie said. And then she had to smile, just a little. "But all right. I don't know where else I would put you except with Hildy Helen, and there is still hope of my turning her into a young lady."

"Not me," Hildy Helen said, grinning and flipping her new bob.

"Hildy?" Dad said, looking at her curiously "Have you done something to your hair?"

The table burst into laughter that was suddenly broken by a shadow that cast itself across the checkered tablecloth. It was Mr. Black Fedora again.

"My employer asked me to make something clear to you, sir," the man said. His voice was flat-sounding.

"What's that?" Dad said, standing up to look him in the eye.

"He appreciates you defendin' one of our own—seein' how the kid's Italian and all that. But it ain't a good idea for a small timer like you to refuse the help of a man like Mr. Capone."

Rudy looked at Little Al. Was he going to jump up and throw open the curtain so he could get a close look at his idol?

Little Al didn't. His face clouded over, and he tugged at Dad's cuff.

"Don't give in to 'em, Mr. Hutchie," he said.

"I don't plan to," Jim Hutchinson said. And to Mr. Black Fedora, he said, "Your 'employer' is merely grateful that my client didn't turn him over lock, stock, and barrel to the police. Be sure he knows it was the boy's own loyalty to his culture that kept him quiet, not anything I did, believe me."

"Still," the man said, eyes glinting viciously, "you may need Mr. Capone's help someday."

"I'll take my chances," Dad said.

As Mr. Black Fedora disappeared inside the curtained booth again, the shadow he'd cast disappeared with him. Perfection returned to the table and within moments everyone was clacking together glasses of Coca-Cola and howling over Little Al's imitation of the evil man.

Rudy took a break from laughing to sit back and draw the scene in his mind.

There was Dad with his pinchy nose and his vague look, who was more of a hero than Tom Mix himself. And there was Hildy Helen. He'd never admit it to her, but he liked her new bob and the way she always stuck by him. And, of course, there was Little Al, his new brother, the one he was going to learn so much from, the one he was going to teach things to as well.

And finally there was Aunt Gussie. She was dryly commenting on Little Al's manners, her eyes narrowed like she was looking through a spyglass at his use of the table napkin. She also had a hint of a smile in her eyes, and she sat back in her chair as if she, too, thought this were a perfect moment.

I wonder if Jesus ever felt like this after He took a risk, Rudy thought from out of the thin air. *I hope He did.*

It might be a good time for a prayer, he decided. And it wasn't even an emergency.

✠ ⬧✠⬧ ✠

Look for Book #2
in THE CHRISTIAN HERITAGE: CHICAGO YEARS series
The Chase

He's mistaken for a truant, he discovers he has to wear glasses, and he has to deal with a playground bully. For Rudy, the school year is off to a terrible start. He dreams of adventure— like joining the circus. Then there's a cross burning in front of the boardinghouse and Little Al turns up missing. Could there be more adventure than Rudy expected in just trying to live like Jesus would?

There's More Adventure in the CHRISTIAN HERITAGE SERIES!

The Salem Years, 1689–1691

The Rescue #1

Josiah Hutchinson's sister Hope is terribly ill. Can a stranger—whose presence could destroy the family's relationship with everyone else in Salem Village—save her?

The Stowaway #2

Josiah's dream of becoming a sailor seems within reach. But will the evil schemes of a tough orphan named Simon land Josiah and his sister in a heap of trouble?

The Guardian #3

Josiah has a plan to deal with the wolves threatening the town. Can he carry it out without endangering himself—or Cousin Rebecca, who'll follow him anywhere?

The Accused #4

Robbed by the cruel Putnam brothers, Josiah suddenly finds himself on trial for crimes he didn't commit. Can he convince anyone of his innocence?

The Samaritan #5

Josiah tries to help a starving widow and her daughter. But will his feud with the Putnams wreck everything he's worked for?

The Secret #6

If Papa finds out who Hope's been sneaking away to see, he'll be furious! Josiah knows her secret; should he tell?

The Williamsburg Years, 1780–1781

The Rebel #1

Josiah's great-grandson, Thomas Hutchinson, didn't rob the apothecary shop where he works. So why does he wind up in jail, and will he ever get out?

The Thief #2

Someone's stealing horses in Williamsburg! But is the masked rider Josiah sees the real culprit, and who's behind the mask?

The Burden #3

Thomas knows secrets he can't share. So what can he do when a crazed Walter Clark holds him at gunpoint over a secret he doesn't even know?

The Prisoner #4

As war rages in Williamsburg, Thomas' mentor refuses to fight and is carried off by the Patriots. Now which side will Thomas choose?

The Invasion #5

Word comes that Benedict Arnold and his men are ransacking plantations. Can Thomas and his family protect their homestead—even when it's invaded by British soldiers who take Caroline as a hostage?

The Battle #6

Thomas is surrounded by war! Can he tackle still another fight, taking orders from a woman he doesn't like—and being forbidden to talk about his missing brother?

The Charleston Years, 1860–1861

The Misfit #1

When the crusade to abolish slavery reaches full swing, Thomas Hutchinson's great-grandson Austin is sent to live with slave-holding relatives. How can he ever fit in?

The Ally #2

Austin resolves to teach young slave Henry-James to read, even though it's illegal. If Uncle Drayton finds out, will both boys pay the ultimate price?

The Threat #3

Trouble follows Austin to Uncle Drayton's vacation home. Who are those two men Austin hears scheming against his uncle—and why is a young man tampering with the family stagecoach?

The Trap #4

Austin's slave friend Henry-James beats hired hand Narvel in a wrestling match. Will Narvel get the revenge he seeks by picking fights and trapping Austin in a water well?

The Hostage #5

As north and south move toward civil war, Austin is kidnapped by men determined to stop his father from preaching against slavery. Can he escape?

The Escape #6

With the Civil War breaking out, Austin tries to keep Uncle Drayton from selling Henry-James at the slave auction. Will it work, and can Austin flee South Carolina with the rest of the Hutchinsons before Confederate soldiers find them?

The Chicago Years, 1928–1929

The Trick #1

Rudy and Hildy Helen Hutchinson and their father move to Chicago to live with their rich great-aunt Gussie. Can they survive the bullies they find—not to mention Little Al, a young schemer with hopes of becoming a mobster?

The Chase #2

Rudy and his family face one problem after another—including an accident that sends Rudy to the doctor, and the disappearance of Little Al. But can they make it through a deadly dispute between the mob and the Ku Klux Klan?

The Capture #3

It's Christmastime, but Rudy finds nothing to celebrate. Will his attorney father's defense of a Jewish boy accused of murder—and Hildy Helen's kidnapping—ruin far more than the holiday?

The Stunt #4

Rudy gets in trouble wing-walking on a plane. But can he stay standing as he finds himself in the middle of a battle for racial equality—and Aunt Gussie's dangerous fight for workers' rights?

The Caper #5

Strange things are going on at Cape Cod, where Rudy and his family are vacationing. What's in a mysterious trunk found on the beach, and who are those shadowy men in a boat who seem to be carrying . . . bodies?

The Pursuit #6

A deadly warning from the mob . . . Aunt Gussie felled by a stroke . . . impending stock market disaster! Rudy just wants to be a kid, but events won't let him. Will his faith be enough to get him through it all?

Available at a Christian bookstore near you

FOCUS ON THE FAMILY®

Like this book?

Then you'll love *Clubhouse* magazine! It's
written for kids just like you, and it's loaded
with great stories, interesting articles, puzzles,
games, and fun things for you to do. Some
issues include posters, too! With
your parents' permission, we'll
even send you a complimentary copy.

Simply write to Focus on the Family, Colorado
Springs, CO 80995 (in Canada, write P.O.
9800, Stn. Terminal, Vancouver, B.C. V6B 4G3) and
mention that you saw this offer in the back of this book. Or,
call 1-800-A-FAMILY (in Canada, call 1-800-661-9800).

You may also visit our Web site (www.family.org) to
learn more about the ministry or find out if there is a
Focus on the Family office in your country.

• • •

"Adventures in Odyssey" is a fantastic series of books, videos, and
radio dramas that's fun for the entire family—parents, too! You'll love
the twists and turns found in the novels, as well as the excitement
packed into every video. And the 30 albums of radio dramas
(available on audiocassette or compact disc) are great to listen to
in the car, after dinner . . . even at bedtime! You can hear
"Adventures in Odyssey" on the radio, too. Call Focus on the
Family for a listing of local stations airing these programs or to
request any of the "Adventures in Odyssey" resources. They're
also available at Christian bookstores everywhere.

*Focus on the Family is an organization that is dedicated to helping you and
your family establish lasting, loving relationships with each other and the Lord.
It's why we exist! If we can assist you or your family in any way,
please feel free to contact us. We'd love to hear from you!*